A
Harlequin
Romance

OTHER

Harlequin Romances

by JOYCE DINGWELL

Many of these titles are available at your local bookseller,
or through the Harlequin Reader Service.

For a free catalogue listing all available Harlequin Romances,
send your name and address to:

HARLEQUIN READER SERVICE,
M.P.O. Box 707, Niagara Falls, N.Y. 14302
Canadian address: Stratford, Ontario, Canada N5A 6W4

or use order coupon at back of books.

THE ROAD BOSS

by

JOYCE DINGWELL

Harlequin Books

TORONTO • LONDON • NEW YORK • AMSTERDAM • SYDNEY • WINNIPEG

Original hardcover edition published in 1976
by Mills & Boon Limited

ISBN 0-373-01998-X

Harlequin edition published August, 1976

Printed in Canada

CHAPTER ONE

IT was a glittering, sun-soaking, heat-dancing day, but, smiled Gemma to the rear-vision mirror of her small car, what else, except when the Wet was on, could you expect from the centre of Australia?

The mirror revealed a long stretch of blue tarred road with a distant blur on it. That blur would be that road train trying to catch up on her again. She believed she had shaken it off at Forty Mile. She grimaced and put her foot down. Its arrogant driver had actually tried to pass her at Forty Mile; that gargantuan monstrosity even had got as far as the monster in the driving cabin being able to look down on her. She had remembered at once what Bruce had warned her about road trains and their operators, and had accelerated sharply. She had kept accelerating until the ogre was left behind. Now it seemed that the fight was on once more.

However, she still had the advantage of a distance of kilos, so there was no immediate panic. Gemma resumed her thoughts.

The rains, only recently finished, had comprised a Wet previously unparalleled up here, or so Godfather had written down, and when Bruce had called on Gemma in Sydney, he had said the same. Godfather had been ecstatic over it all. The intense rains had uncovered remarkable data for a scientist, he had gloated. Bruce on the other hand had been distinctly

5

less than enthusiastic. It had been good to see the waterholes filled, he had admitted, but a lot of his cattle had been bogged and had to be dug out; also because of the resultant floods there had been a delay in road training the beasts south.

The mobs no longer were driven overland, Bruce had explained, but were trucked in road trains down The Bitumen, much less spectacular, for overlanding was a grand scale undertaking, but far more economical and reliable. There had always been big stock losses on the hoof, and it had taken a deuce of a time, whereas road transport entailed only minor losses and was certainly fast. Oh, yes, Bruce had told Gemma, trucking the beasts instead of droving them was the lesser of two evils. He had said this last with emphasis. He had made no secret of his dislike of truckies, or, as he had told Gemma they were known in the Centre, the road bosses.

Now this particular road boss was giving Gemma a go for it a second time. The distant blur had grown to a less distant smudge. Down went Gemma's foot again.

The jerk forward upset the balance of the carefully spread-out gown encased in cellophane occupying the entire back seat. Muttering angrily, Gemma pulled up the car and put the dress back again. It wasted precious time, but it was, after all, very precious. It was her wedding gown. When she resumed again, the blur that had grown into a smudge had now grown into a shape. A road train shape. However, it was still a long way off.

All the girls in the office had envied Gemma her need to take to her marriage with Bruce only a wed-

6

ding gown. (She was also taking a cake, likewise made by her own hands, but that was to be her surprise.) No linen to be transported. No six of this or dozen of that. No saucepans. Bruce already had plenty.

The girls also had envied Gemma the speed of things. Two weeks getting to know each other, then an engagement ring, then later Gemma hitting west with a view to marriage.

"Tony and I have had an 'understanding' for ages," Noni had sighed.

"We're waiting for two years," Jean had complained.

They had called it whirlwind, yet it wasn't, not really. Bruce had proved himself a fast wind, but he didn't exactly whirl you off your feet. He didn't sweep you. He wasn't the type, and anyway . . . and a frank grin from Gemma . . . wasn't she turned twenty-six and past sweeping?

"I'm twenty-six," Gemma said to the mirror . . . the shape was quite clear now . . . "and at twenty-six you don't get whirled or swept."

She had been very proud of Bruce, though. Tall, nicely tanned, extremely polished. She had said to him at their first encounter : "You don't seem like an outback man."

"I was years at college, remember," he had answered with a distinct college accent, and had proceeded in that college accent to deliver Godfather's message along with Godfather's letter.

"Do you see Godfather, then ?" Gemma had asked, fingering the letter.

"Rudhill Scientific Block is only some hundred kilos from us, almost next door, you might say." Bruce had smiled as he had said it to Gemma. "No, I don't meet the scientists and geologists and what-have-yous at all, as a matter of fact we pastoralists don't always see eye to eye with them, but when they found out I was coming down to Sydney, and believe me, everything is found out by the grapevine up there, and was asked to contact you, I could scarcely refuse." A pause. "I'm very glad I didn't refuse . . . *now*."

It had been such a flattering confession that Gemma had not thought about the possible alternative for Bruce, that of refusing Godfather. She had simply said: "Thank you. I'm glad, too," and felt quite exalted. She had added, coming back to earth: "But what can it all be about?"

"Perhaps the letter—" Bruce had prompted charmingly, and Gemma had nodded.

"Of course, the letter." She had opened Godfather's note.

She had always called Bernard Drews that, called him Godfather. He *was* her godfather, and since her own father was dead . . . her mother, too . . . the little girl she had been when it all had happened had yearned for someone nearer than just "Mr. Drews" or even "Uncle Bernard". Small Gemma had wanted a father.

"I *am* your father," Bernard Drews had insisted. "I'm your godfather. Call me Godfather."

"Yes, Godfather," Gemma had said eagerly.

Bernard Drews was a scientist. Growing up, Gemma had seen very little of him, he had either been down in Antarctica or somewhere on the equator, but it hadn't mattered, he always came back, and he always loved her, and she always loved him. Currently he was north of the Centre, proving occurrences of Permian rock, the palaeozoic and the carboniferous systems, if you understood what that meant. Gemma didn't.

Others in Rudhill Scientific Block photographed cosmic rays, or were geo-physicists, or wolfram and mica men, which Gemma did not understand, either. She simply classed them all fondly as Brains. But fondest of all, of course, Godfather.

She had opened the folded paper.

"It's to ask me to look out an old prescription of Godfather's, have it dispensed, then take it up when I go." Gemma had looked worried. Godfather was getting on now. Was he as well as he always declared he was?

"You're going up there?" Bruce had said. . . . Bruce Mannering, she had learned by now . . . with interest. "When?"

"In a month."

"If only I could wait that long I could take you myself, but you know how it is on the land."

Gemma had not known, apart from holidays at odd places wherever Godfather happened to be, she was a Sydney girl. But she had murmured: "Yes."

"I would have loved that," he had said eagerly, and at once had added: "As it can't be, at least let us see as much as we can of each other before I go."

"*I* would love that." It had been Gemma's turn to be eager.

It had been a fabulous fortnight. She and Bruce had gone everywhere, done everything. Then, to top it all, especially as regarded the girls in the office, Bruce had proposed.

Flattered, a little intoxicated with herself and her success after Noni's envious moans and Jean's wistfulness, also quite in love with six feet of handsome, tanned, obviously well-to-do manhood, for who wouldn't be? Gemma had said Yes. The only thing that nice Bruce had insisted on had been marriage up there, not here.

"You have no people here in Sydney, Gemma, but a godfather close to Mannering Park" ... Mannering Park was the Mannering stronghold ... "while I have all my people up there, so naturally up there it must be."

"Yes," Gemma had agreed.

She had been a little regretful, for she had wanted to show Bruce off to the girls, Bruce with his polish and his good looks and his utter eligibility. Still, she had had to agree that up there made sense.

"You'll fly, of course, dear," Bruce had said next.

"No, I'll drive. You see, Bruce, I know I have nothing to take—I mean, no six of this, no dozen of that. I know Mannering Park has everything because you've told me, but there's still my books, a few odds and ends I value, and" ... a dimple ... "my wedding gown. Unless you don't want me dressed up."

"Of course I want you dressed up. All the Top End—well, all the Top End who matter—will be there. Planes will come from hundreds and hundreds of miles. Mother wouldn't have anything less."

"Your mother lives at Mannering Park, too?"

"All the Mannerings. We're a self-contained little world. But don't think you'll be on top of anybody, dear, the bungalows are at least several miles apart."

"Oh," Gemma had said, relieved.

"Mother will love to have you in the family homestead until we're married," Bruce had continued.

"No, I don't think so," Gemma had declined cautiously.

"But, my dear, it would be hardly the thing for you to come to my house. I mean, not before."

"Before?"

"Before the wedding, Gemma."

"Even up there?" Gemma had disbelieved. Surely, she had been thinking, in this day and age—

"*Especially* up there. We're sticklers, Gemma. So it will have to be Mother's."

"No, it will be Godfather's. I'll be married from Godfather's."

"From barracks?"

"They're not, actually, they're a block of very private units, where everyone keeps well to himself. I mean, Bruce, a cosmic ray man would have nothing in common with a geologist, and a rock man like Godfather—well, he's the freakiest of all." Gemma had laughed fondly. "No," she had said seriously, "it's not a barracks, it's a set of villas, and ours—Bernard Drews'—is so far away you can't see the others."

"Interesting," Bruce had nodded, obviously not interested, and Gemma had not blamed him. Permian rock was not exactly something that kept you on your toes.

"Well, dear," he had said presently, "if you want to be married from Rudhill, that's all right with me. And after all, it does concede to the conventions. But if you must drive up—"

"Yes, I must." Gemma had said it a little abstractedly, she had been thinking of those "conventions".

"Then," had continued Bruce, "I'll give you some advice. Do it in easy stages. Book accommodation ahead; these times no one stops out at night, it can be dangerous. Always keep your petrol topped, it can be disastrous out there to run dry. Most of all, and I repeat *most of all*, watch the road trains."

"Are they that bad?" Gemma had disbelieved.

"They'd be bad enough on wide concrete, but on narrow tar they are a catastrophe. It's the drivers. They're ruthless, forthright, greedy, overbearing, presumptuous, spiteful, and really not far from savages."

"Yet they do have a road right, too."

"Not as much as they take."

"But they have a wide load," she pointed out.

"And demand a wider share of the tar. Please heed me, Gemma. Take every precaution with a road train, and particularly the driver of the train. Road bosses, they're called ... and incidentally, they call us the terrorists."

"Terrorists?"

"Changed from tourists. Everyone in a private car is a tourist and thus a terrorist to them."

"Perhaps they've had a bad time with tourists."

"To my mind it couldn't be bad enough," Bruce had said.

"Will I have a bad time with tourists, Bruce?" Gemma had mused. "I mean, tourists do wander across the road looking at things."

"They'll be few around at this time of the year, especially after the recent bad weather. No, your only hazard will be the thirty-six-wheelers."

"Thirty-six-wheelers?" she queried.

"The road trains."

"Why do you call them that?"

"Because, counting their spares, they have thirty-six wheels."

"What else about them, Bruce?"

"The vehicles are three-fifty horse-power, and I mean horse, not ponies. They have no timetable, their orders from their superiors are 'Do it as quick as you can' meaning, of course, as quick as you can *regardless*. Now do you follow me, Gemma?"

"Oh, yes, yes, I do." Gemma had shivered.

"So, dear, for my sake, for your own sake, watch out for them, for I can assure you they won't watch out for you, not a mere terrorist."

"Thank you for warning me, Bruce."

"Just remember the warning, Gemma."

"Oh, I will."

Gemma glanced back at the shape again, now three shapes, three monstrous trucks fastened together in articulation, a lofty cabin in the foremost articulation, and she did as Bruce had requested. She remembered.

Her foot went down to the boards and stayed there. The country raced past her, though she knew that actually she was racing past it. It was indescribably beautiful, as Godfather always insisted, really heart-thudding in its intense vitality, stunning in its Egyptian pottery colours. There was flame, magenta, purple, ochre, orange, violet. Something, too, had happened since the rains. Green had crept in—a vivid pulsing green, but flaunting through the green was something even more breathless. It was the shouting blue of the Salvation Jane. The Jane spread everywhere, the bluest blue, Gemma thought quite stunned with the explosion of colour, in all the world.

Her absorption in the landscape had made her forget to check on the road train, but now she did. Good grief, the savage . . . yes, Bruce had been right, *savage* . . . was almost on her bumper bars. And now the fool was blowing a monstrous horn.

She had as much right to the road as he had, but all the same she was not going to act the idiot and be squashed. Angrily, resentfully, but inevitably, she edged off the tar on to the dirt verge. All right, savage, it's all yours, she cried out.

But the savage only did what he had done before, he brought the cabin equal to her steering wheel and looked down on her. In the few seconds she allowed herself to take her eyes off the road, Gemma saw very white teeth in a very brown face, not Bruce's pleasant golden tan, but leather brown. She saw blue eyes deep-set as the eyes of men who look long and far into the distance usually are. She had no time for any more impressions, for now the man was screaming at her. Of all things he was ordering:

"Pull up! Stop!"

Now Gemma's foot almost went through the floor boards. I'll show him! she seethed. Boss of the road, is he? Well, boss, you're in for a shock.

But it was Gemma who was shocked, not the driver. She never would have credited that a thirty-six-wheeler, an articulated monstrosity, could reach such a speed. The thing went past her almost as though she was stationary. She had a vague impression of cattle, then more cattle, then more again. Then when the monster reached an accommodating several hundred yards ahead, it slewed round and cut her off.

She saw it turn, and she guessed the intention, but even then she refused to credit it. No man would do a thing like that. But . . . a faint fear creeping in . . . a savage would.

She braked.

She should have braked earlier, but she still had not believed that what looked like happening actually would happen. The final halt was only accomplished a bare inch from the great monster.

At once the savage was out of his cabin and coming thundering down at her.

"What in tarnation do you think you're doing?" he shouted. "Didn't you hear me tell you to stop?"

"Yes," she came back, equally thunderous, "but though you're boss of the road, you're not boss of me!"

He glared at her, but he did not follow it up, not then. "We'll see about that later," he said. "Meanwhile you have a passenger."

"A passenger?"

"Yes."

"Not—you!"

"No. I'll fetch it down. I haven't room for it in my driving cabin because it's plumbfull of gear already. But you have an empty car."

"I have not!"

"Well, you have room at least for one small fellow. Fellow-ess, to be exact. It's a girl."

"It's a— What on earth are you talking about?"

"A calf has been dropped." He jerked his head towards the articulated trucks.

"Dropped? Dropped where? Was it hurt?"

"Oh, for heaven's sake, don't you know the birds and the bees bit?"

"Of course."

"Then a calf has been born. If I leave it there, it'll be dead in five minutes. It will be trampled on. I haven't an inch to spare myself."

"But I can't take a calf," she protested.

"Well, you can't abandon it out here."

"You—you shouldn't have accepted a pregnant cow."

"Look, lady" ... with heavy patience ... "the number of beasts in that load would stagger you. It takes us all our time to load them, let alone ask them individually, the females, I mean, if they're in a certain delicate condition."

"Well, I still can't take it. I'm making for Alice Springs for the night."

"So am I. I'll meet up with you and Harriet there."

"Why Harriet?"

"Well, she's not a Harry, is she?"

"It's quite impossible. All my trousseau is on the back seat and my cake is on the front." But Gemma was talking to air; the man had run off.

He was a giant of a man, she saw angrily, as huge among men as his monstrosity would be huge among ordinary trucks. He was also just as Bruce had warned: ruthless, forthright, greedy, overbearing, presumptuous, spiteful. But, gritted Gemma, she'd soon put him in his place.

She thought how satisfactory it would be to say to this low savage: "I am Mrs. Mannering of Mannering Park, and I can tell you now, my man, that you'll never truck for us."

But hardly had that very pleasant, very irresistible thought occurred than he occurred again, carrying a bundle this time that looked all legs and head. Before she could stop him, he had opened the passenger door and deposited the calf on the passenger seat, which would have been bad enough had it been empty, for no one wants to drive beside a calf passenger, but holding as it did a large white cake. . . .

"My cake!" yelped Gemma, and looked aghast at lovers' knots and silver horseshoes and almond icing flying everywhere.

"Sorry," he said, actually a little discountenanced, and leaning over he promptly lifted Harriet and plopped her in the back.

Then, before Gemma could cry out again, he went.

She watched him in silence. Something had happened to her throat. Also her voice wasn't working any more. She saw the road train take off and was still silent, then she followed it into the distance until it was not there at all, and was still dumb.

Then slowly, disbelievingly, she came to life again. She turned.

The calf was still where the savage had deposited it, and that was across the back seat. *And on her dress.*

When he had put it down, he must have torn the cellophane dust-cover and—well, the calf had done the rest.

There sat Harriet in a drift of white chiffon with lace overlay. The filmy veil Gemma had packed with the gown had somehow come adrift, somehow caught on two sticky calf ears, still wet from birth, and now Harriet actually wore a bridal wreath. It only needed a flower in a hoof and Harriet would be ready to walk down an aisle, Gemma thought hysterically, and as though she read that thought, Harriet reached out at that moment and helped herself to a candied lovers' knot from the front seat, making the chiffon tear from end to end.

It was then that Gemma's long silence broke at last. She wept.

CHAPTER TWO

IN between her streaming tears Gemma could see the calf staring solemnly at her. Harriet had big plum eyes with a luxurious fringe of silky lashes. Her nose was moist, black and india-rubbery. Her ears were really something, soft and peaked and covered with downy gold hair, the insides of the ears were pink plush. She wore that irresistible cherubic expression that toymakers toil long to achieve on their cuddly animal offerings, since a child must be won at a first encounter.

Now Gemma was won.

"You're beautiful," she said, the tears drying saltily on her face, "I'd like to put a bell round your neck for you to wear for a locket." She had put her hand out to the calf as she spoke, and Harriet licked it with a lolly pink tongue.

The sugar lovers' knot the calf had taken had proved strange to her taste, and she had discarded it, but not before its powder had landed above her mouth. Harriet now wore a very cute moustache.

"I can't keep you, of course," Gemma told the little thing, laughing now instead of crying, "not even until we get to The Alice, as *he* arranged, but before I tumble you out into the mulga you can have the milk I brought for my tea."

She found her picnic hamper and withdrew the bottle of milk she had had filled at Forty Mile.

"You don't know it yet, Harriet," she said, "but you're what's called a poddy calf." She put her finger in the bottle and brought the bottle up close to the calf's mouth, then proceeded to fill Harriet up.

It took a very long time. A road train went past, then two tourists. What had Bruce said the savages called them? Oh, yes, terrorists.

One of the tourists nearly went off the road staring at her. Anyone would think, said Gemma crossly to Harriet, that they had never seen a calf fed before. In her indignation it did not occur to her to tack on that they might never have seen a calf dressed in a wedding gown and veil being poddy-fed on the back seat of a car before.

"Actually you should be fed like this for a week," Gemma said next to Harriet, "and after that you should graze. But I'm afraid, my dear, in your case—"

It was a long time before the bottle was finished, and in that time something happened to Gemma. Though, she thought wryly, it would have happened even without the long . . . and thought-permitting . . . time it took to feed the calf. For in the end she knew she would never have discarded Harriet. Who could have tumbled out such a plum-eyed, rubber-nosed, small thing?

She took off the veil, though, and the torn dress, and she wiped off the ridiculous sugar moustache. Then she got behind the wheel and started off again, next stop Alice Springs . . . and what, oh, what were people going to say at a car with a calf as a passenger?

Harriet went to sleep and once more Gemma ate up the miles, the Egyptian pottery colours flashing past like the facets in a kaleidoscope, the new green grass flaunting at her, the explosion of Salvation Jane almost hurting her eyes with its blue.

Then the first signs of closer settlement began, and in the far distance Gemma could see the McDonnell Ranges that parted at Heavitree Gap to cradle the very centre of Australia at Alice Springs.

She glanced back at Harriet, and she was sound asleep now, and slunk so low she was barely noticeable.

"Stay like that," she implored. "We're now in civilization, roads and footpaths and even an arcade, I'm told. A really mod hotel."

She turned into Todd Street.

The fine lawns of the fine houses being kept fresh and green by sprinklers (though just now after the Wet there was less need for watering) made Gemma a little uneasy. The savage had called out that he would meet up with them at The Alice, but, glancing again at the suburban-like setting, it appeared barely the kind of place where you could pull up at an imposing sweep of hotel stairs and step out with a newborn calf.

She found and approached the hotel gingerly, and was just about to do a street circuit to find a back entrance when she saw the hateful road train.

It was his—the savage's. She did not recognize it by its name since the Territorian Transport that was written on it had not registered on her before, but she did remember the man. Even if she hadn't, she would still have had to stop. He came out and stepped right in front of her, just like he had halted his monstrosity in front of her a few hours earlier, and the only way she could have avoided him would have been to run over him. Which, she fumed, might not have been such a bad idea!

He crossed to her window, and when she did not lean out to listen to him, he leaned inwards to her.

"If you hand out the spoil," he said, "I'll take over the responsibility of Harriet, leaving you to climb the front stairs as an elegant lady should."

"No," Gemma replied.

"No?" His thick brows had risen steeply, making him look quite an austere aristocrat, if a man in a black sweatshirt and oil-stained denims could ever look that.

"I'm keeping her," Gemma said. She had not thought about it before, but now, all at once, she did, and she was quite resolved.

"Oh, come off it," he said, "she's not a pet poodle."

"I know, but she's been given to me, so now she's mine."

"She's not!" he retorted.

"Well, she's not yours."

"She could be if I kept quiet about the blessed event—after all, I signed for X number of beasts, not X and a half. But Territorian doesn't do things that way."

"Territorian?"

He nodded to the road train taking up all the street, and particularly at its sign: Territorian Transport.

"You work for Territorian?" asked Gemma.

"No, Territorian works for me."

Gemma gave an impatient hunch of her shoulders. "It's the same thing."

He did not argue that. But he did lean right in to

take up the calf.

"No," Gemma said again, "I—I like her."

"Even after tearing your dress?" He had left the scene before he had witnessed the damage, but he must have noticed the tatters of material now.

"You, not the calf, did that," she told him coldly.

"I suppose next you'll be blaming me for the cake as well. Why in Betsy did you bring a cake? Bringing a cake up here would be like taking coals to Newcastle. All the Inside ladies are dab hands at cake. Ever heard of country cooking?"

Gemma did not answer that last, but she did reply to the first question.

"It was a very special cake."

"Don't tell me, let me guess. It was a christening cake. You knew *before* about Harriet."

"Don't be stupid, how could I know? It"... Gemma paused... "was a wedding cake." Another pause. "My wedding cake. I'm getting married up here."

"Go on." The man leaned even further in. "Do I know him?"

"How would I know that?"

"I know everyone from Adelaide to Maree to The Alice to Darwin, except, of course, the passers-through."

"Well, Bruce isn't that."

"Bruce?"

"Look, it's no business of yours, but to hurry things up, for I do want a bath before dinner, it's Mr. Bruce Mannering of Mannering Park."

The savage looked long at Gemma, and then he said one rude incredulous word. He said:

"Struth!"

"I beg your pardon?"

"It doesn't matter," he dismissed, "except that *now*, more than ever, you can't take Harriet in there."

"I wasn't taking her in there, only leaving her in some safe place near there, but why do you say now more than ever?"

"Because," he said cryptically, "you'll soon find out that they, so eventually you, just don't."

"I do believe I can read something in that," Gemma retorted. "I believe you've had dealings with the Mannerings and they've put you in your place."

"And what place is that?"

"Road boss, a ruthless, forthright, greedy, overbearing, presumptuous, spiteful thirty-six-wheeler, not all that far from a savage . . . Mr. Territorian, you're hurting me! Let go my arm at once!"

"I'd like to break it," he said, but he still released her. "No, I haven't had dealings with the Mannerings . . . well, not that kind, not the road kind. The Mannerings are not my customers. Bagsworth trucks for them."

Although she would have liked to have learned *what* kind of dealings, Gemma brought the subject back to Harriet.

"What can I do with her tonight?" she appealed.

"Ask at the desk for a double bed."

"Be serious!"

"If I were, you wouldn't sit down for a week, not after the things you just said."

Gemma looked indignantly at him.

"Why are you going on like this?" she demanded. "It's I who've been imposed on, not you. You give

24

me the little girl, then you expect me to hand her over like—like an animal!"

The absurdity of her statement did not occur to Gemma until he reminded her: "Well, she is, you know." He grinned, but Gemma found she could not smile back.

"You're going to take her for veal," she accused. "That's what they do with young cattle, don't they, make them vealers."

"As a matter of fact my idea was to graze her for twelve months, then sell her for a yearling. Choice meat, yearling. You can name your own price. Of course if one takes a liking to a beast and keeps it five years . . . store cattle it's called then . . . there's always the hamburger market. Now *you're* hurting me." For Gemma had wound up the window to cut out his hateful voice and had not stopped at the big brown fingers fastened across the glass top. But she did stop winding at his protest, and putting his arm over he reversed the window down again.

"How can you feed Harriet?" he asked.

"Poddy-feed her."

"Oh, so you know that?"

"Of course I know that."

He paused a moment.

"You haven't any ideas of rearing her for future milk, have you, for she'll never be that kind of cow. I mean, she could feed a calf of her own some day, but there it would stop. This breed is not like a Jersey, it has small udders. Also" . . . a small lopsided smile . . . "you would need a bull."

"As you asked me and as I told you," she reminded thinly, "I do know the birds and the bees bit."

25

"Rather awkward if you didn't," he nodded, "with a marriage coming up."

"Look here, Mr. Territorian—"

"Just Territorian will do, or better still Tim. I'm Tim Torrance. Very few get called Mister up here."

"I think," resumed Gemma frozenly, "this conversation has gone far enough."

"It hasn't even started yet. You're asking me what to do, how to go about it, then promptly not listening. Well, right now I'll bed Harriet somewhere at the back, and you can walk up the front stairs like an elegant lady should." He added: "An elegant Mannering."

"That doesn't solve things."

"It will—if you give me a moment. Go in and register, then meet me at dinner and we'll thrash it all out. I've already booked in myself."

"*You* have booked in!"

He must have read her complete amazement, for he looked back at her and grinned.

"Takes your breath, doesn't it? But see here, Future Mrs. Mannering, you are not now in Sydney, climbing the stairs of the Hilton or the Wentworth, you are in the dead centre, and here it doesn't count whether you went to college or bush school, or whether you wear an imported Savile Row suit or local working clobber."

"The same clobber," said Gemma deliberately, eyeing his stains and grease and sweat, "as you wore since that bush school."

"Not exactly. I had short pants then, but the sweatshirt could be the same."

"Yes—unwashed." She murmured it quietly, yet

26

he still heard her.

But instead of tackling her, he merely grinned again. "You'll be surprised," he said, "how I clean up. Now you go along and send down a porter for your bags and I'll put the baby to bed." He opened the door and edged Gemma out, put her bags on the sidewalk, put his hand forward for the car keys, then started and drove the car to some back way she must have missed.

For a vexed moment Gemma just stood, then with a shrug she went up the hotel stairs.

"Name of Glasson," she said at the desk. "I booked a room by mail."

"Certainly, Miss Glasson. We've been expecting you. Mr. Torrance said you were on the way."

"Mr. Torrance? He would be—"

"The Territorian, yes. Lionel, bring in the bags, then room seventeen for Miss Glasson."

Before Gemma could ask any more questions, she was whisked away to a very tasteful and very abundant room.

It was a room even big enough, she thought, looking around, for a double occupancy, just as he, that savage who worked for Territorian, had suggested. A double bed, she had been told, for herself and Harriet.

What a man!

She began taking things out of her case.

It was heaven just to lie in the bath and soak. Evidently the manager understood the bone weariness of travelling in the centre, for the tub was king size and bath salts had been provided. Also the towels were thick thirsty ones, and generous in number.

Gemma lay back and began to feel a little better.

She wondered idly how the savage would "clean up", then decided unkindly to make a fool of him tonight and to wear simply everything for dinner. At the most, she thought, a man like that, a thirty-six-wheeler even though he was a road boss, could carry only another pair of pants and another shirt.

She got out of the bath at last and went through her dresses, all beautiful brand-new dresses as befitted a bride. She decided devilishly on a particularly lavish, long patio silk ... that should floor him ... and dressed leisurely and carefully. She was sorry she could not add her engagement ring, but Bruce had that. Bruce had said that most certainly his mother would want a formal engagement dinner, so he had taken it with him. "As I told you, Gemma, the Mannerings are sticklers," Bruce had smiled. Gemma looked regretfully at her bare finger now, took a long, last, satisfied look at herself and decided that the tawny shades of the flowers in the silk did things to her slightly tawny blonde hair and matching eyes, then decided to go down.

When she reached the stairs and looked over the balustrade, she was a little bit piqued to see that *he* had not put in an appearance yet. She had rather fancied the turning of his head at her approach ... stairs were so spectacular ... then the crestfallen look at his own gear after hers. Now, she thought, impressed, if only he had presented the sartorial perfection of the man already standing there, standing in a semi-formal grey flannel, stark white shirt, tasteful striped tie, then it would be entirely different. But that man knew what to wear, and undoubtedly was accustomed to wearing it. He also knew some impressive women. The girl he was with was really outstanding. She also, and Gemma noted it a little crossly, had let her head go, as Gemma had, in tonight's dress. If anything, she outdid Gemma. However . . . a shrug . . . the pair had nothing to do, either of them, with her or the savage. At that moment the man turned, and Gemma flinched.

It *was* the Territorian.

That was Gemma's first shock. The second was that he *had* cleaned up well. He had cleaned up—quite remarkably.

All this she thought in a split minute. In the other part of the minute she actually was in the road boss's arms. Right in them. Enclosed in them.

"Darling," he was saying very distinctly, "you've been hours, but it's been worth every second." He held her back from him and looked admiringly at her. Then very deliberately and very unmistakably and very intentionally, he kissed her.

"Dinner is waiting," he said, and Gemma found herself being shepherded to the dining room, being ushered to a corner table for two, being plied with wine.

The same as when he had left her with the calf, she had something the matter with her throat and her voice wouldn't work. But when it did return this time, she did not cry. She said:

"Are you quite mad?"

"The classic answer they tell me is Yes, mad for you, but that would be asking for it, wouldn't it, from the future wife of a Mannering."

"She—that girl—will think—"

"Yes?"

"She'll think that I'm your—your—"

"Mistress, fiancée or wife," he nodded. "That was the purpose. Any of the three would do so long as she got the message that you belonged."

"Belonged?" she echoed.

"To me. And don't say I'm crazy any more. I know her sort."

"What sort?"

"Bush Bettys doing the rounds and hoping for some mug."

"Bush Bettys?" she queried.

"That's my tag. Centre Claras, if you like, or Territory Tessies. Anyway, girls out for a nice return."

"You mean *you*?"

"Any mug. As I would be one if I fell."

"But why would she be interested in you?"

"Am I that bad?"

"No, but—"

"I'm also not exactly penniless, and you may not have noticed the tourist boutique in the vestibule where we were standing, but there were some very valuable opals there."

"You don't mean—"

"I do mean. And why not? Am I that repulsive, then, even with money?"

"No," she admitted, "and you have cleaned up well. But—"

"But?"

"Would a girl like that go for a man like you? She was very elegant, very tasteful. Quite a beauty. Oh, I have no doubt you earn a good wage, I've often read how much, but wouldn't an adventuress, as I think they call them, go for a—boss?"

"I am a boss."

"I know, but I didn't mean just a road boss."

"Then I'll go a little further. I'm boss *of* the road bosses. Yes, that's right." She must be looking disbelieving, Gemma thought, and indeed, she did disbelieve. "The outfit belongs to me. I'm the Territorian himself."

"You are?" she gasped.

"Yes."

"Then why—"

"Why was I driving? I do that occasionally, I never let myself lose touch."

"But would she know that?"

"Out here, everyone knows everything. You'll soon find that out."

"And you say that she would be aware that you are—"

"Tim Torrance of Territorian Transport. I say, that's quite a tongue-twister, isn't it? Yes, ma'am, she would know just that. And now if you don't mind, Future Mrs. Mannering, I'd like to start my nosh."

He did start, but for a while Gemma simply sat there.

"You are a savage, aren't you?" she said at last.

"I use a knife and fork," he returned. "But don't be misled. If the meat's tough, I'll still take it to the mat and gnaw over it like Fido. Now start, please. I'm not going to embarrass you. I won't take up any bones and I won't spill the gravy."

"You're impossible!" she snapped.

"You," he said, "are beautiful."

She looked across at him, startled ... and was startled at the look he gave back. It was a very, very long look.

At twenty-six, Gemma thought incredulously, you don't get looked at like that.

She glanced away, and presently he started talking, and in relief at first, and then in very real interest, Gemma talked back.

"I used to overland the mobs," the man said, "and it's really the only way, but, the same as many things now, the family round the kitehen table of a night working under the big lamp, for instance, it's not with us any more. Like going blackberrying, like—"

"Like going mushrooming," came in Gemma.

"Like Sunday School anniversaries and singing 'All Things Bright and Beautiful'," he tacked on.

"Or 'Bringing in the Sheaves'," added Gemma. "Though," she said a little shyly, "I think you still sing." Gemma had been drinking the wine he had plied, but it was not just that making her suddenly able to express herself. "I think you sang on those overland treks," she told him.

"An overlander has to sing the cattle," he reminded her.

"Sing the cattle?"

"Singing the cattle means soothing them to sleep."

"But you have cattle on your trailers, too."

"Packed so tightly," he said sadly, "there wouldn't be room for one note. However, those overlanding days are past."

"Did you go straight into road trains?" she asked him.

"Future Mrs. Mannering, road trains are in the millionaire category. No, I did not. I toiled for years on trucks." He grinned reminiscently.

"Were they that funny?" She had seen his remembering grin.

"They were always interesting. I picked up a lone hiker one day because he carried a guitar and I rather fancied a song. But from nowhere it seems a whole group appeared, and I got all the music, full blast, that I wanted."

"Tell me more," she invited.

"I'd like to *show* you more," he said. "Ever slept in the cabin behind the steering wheel?"

"No."

"It's wonderful, Future Mrs. Mannering. There you are aloft in your safe eyrie, far up where no one can break the fortress, and if you look out at midnight you'll see star shadows. Ever seen star shadows?"

"No," said Gemma again, thinking how wonderful it would be.

"Then we must show you some time."

"Perhaps." Gemma added a little hurriedly: "Tell me about now. About the thirty-six-wheelers."

"I own twenty road trains," he said quite casually, "more than that of trucks, plus a fleet of little beetles to run up and down The Bitumen and be general trouble-shooters for both." He took a long slow drink. "I saw what was coming and got in quick."

"And ruthlessly, I would think," she suggested.

"Well, I didn't stand back and say 'You first'. There's a team of two on every haul, and they're changed at a prescribed time. It's not an easy livelihood, road bossing, far from it. For instance you have to stop every fifty miles and charge up any fallen cattle, otherwise they'd die by being trampled on."

"How do you mean charge?" she asked.

"A charger is used."

"Not a——"

"Yes, an electric charger. Something to get him or her on their feet in a hurry, otherwise they're history. It's the only way. If you did it with a stick it would be cruel."

"It would also," said Gemma distastefully, "bruise the meat for the abattoirs."

There was a silence for a while. The Territorian broke it. "Well, you did ask me," he reminded her.

"Yes. I'm sorry, it isn't your fault. Do any of your men have hallucinations? I mean, one often reads about that, reads how they work so hard they imagine things and often finish up on the other side of the road."

"If they do, if *mine* do," he said grimly, "it's their own damn fault. I pay them a top wage."

"Yet you keep no timetable, you tell them to be as quick as they can." Gemma remembered that from Bruce, though Bruce, she recalled, had added a significant "regardless".

"No, I don't keep a timetable, but no, also, I don't tell them to be as quick as they can. Some might ... and do. The Territorian doesn't. It pays well, very well, but it doesn't pay extra for fast returns. Next question, please."

"Are tourists 'terrorists'?"

"Yes. They're also fiends. They forget we're twice their size, sometimes three times, and even reverse it by taking twice and three times their due themselves."

"Are mobs better moved quicker? I mean, travelling leisurely surely is still the better way."

"The nicer way, but not better."

"Does a man have to be a different sort of man to be a road boss?"

"Any man would have to be different driving a thing of that size through the middle of nowhere sometimes for five months at a stretch."

"But how different?" she persisted.

"Just a little case of being born with a steering wheel in his hand." He smiled across at her, his teeth very white in his leather brown face. "Coffee is served in the vestibule, Miss Interrogator. As you sip it you can see what the tourist shop has to offer. Ready, Future Mrs. Mannering?"

"You do go on ridiculously." Gemma rose, a little annoyed. She had been miles away in a world of star shadows, and she didn't like coming to earth.

"But accurately?" He had taken it that she referred to his "Future Mrs. Mannering". He added: "You *are* marrying the guy?"

"We're engaged," she said stiffly.

"That's not an answer. Incidentally, I see no ring."

"Bruce has the ring."

"Handy," he grinned.

"Handy?" Gemma queried.

"You could do what our Bush Betty did, or tried to do—win yourself a second ring."

"One is enough, thank you," she said coldly.

"If you have it."

"Oh, I have it."

He had come behind her to help her up. "I'll take your word for that."

There were quite a few people in the vestibule; hidden in the corner of the dining room Gemma had not seen the number of patrons. Balancing their coffee, the guests were all absorbed now in what offered in the tourist display.

Gemma joined them, Tim Torrance close behind her, and she expressed interest in nulla-nullas, waddies, didgeridoos, tribal paintings.

But most of all the opals. You simply could not look away from the opals.

"There are black opals and white opals," Tim Torrance was saying over her shoulder, "and both are misnomers. Black are really fire, flame, sunrise and sunset mixed together, and white are maidens' dreams. Are you a maiden, Harriet's rescuer?"

"I'm twenty-six, so I could scarcely be categorized as a maiden any longer," Gemma said, annoyed. Really, this man!

"Then it's a black for you." Before Gemma knew what he was doing, he was prompting her into the boutique.

She tried to protest. She tried to turn away.

"I'll take it back afterwards," he whispered in her ear, "but right now Betty is watching us. Accept it, for heaven's sake, then reward me with a kiss."

"I can't!"

"It's a beauty." He nodded to the display.

"I still can't. Mr. Torrance ... Territorian ... I'm *engaged*."

"I said I'd take it back afterwards."

"But—"

"We both like this one," said the man to the attendant, and a magnificent ring was being persuaded

36

down Gemma's finger. The third finger of her left hand.

"I can't," she tried again.

"Be quiet, our friend is hanging on every word. If you let me down I'm a doomed man."

"But—"

"With all my love, darling." The Territorian had raised his voice a decibel, he could not help being heard. He was coming close to Gemma again, kissing her again since she had not stepped forward, as ordered, to kiss him. Only there was something different about his kiss now. Or—or was it *her*? Gemma thought.

For, in spite of herself, she was leaning forward to be kissed again, leaning forward intentionally, and the things that she had said were past twenty-six were happening. It was impossible, but they still were happening. Rainbows. Tiptoe. Cloud nine. Being "swept".

"You never said," he whispered, still breath-close to her, "what your name was, Future Mrs. Mannering."

"Glasson," she told him.

"Before that?"

"Gemma." He repeated it after her. Then he said:

"And how long does Bruce Mannering think he can keep this gem in a box?"

CHAPTER THREE

A MAID wakened Gemma the next morning with a
breakfast tray with a note propped against the coffee
pot. When she had left, Gemma opened the envelope
and saw that the message was from the Territorian.

"Good morning, Future Mrs. Mannering. By the
time you read this I'll have been on the road for
hours, but not in your direction, so don't think you
can catch me."—Catch him, indeed!—"I've instruc-
ted the hotel yard man to install Harriet when you're
ready to leave. You should be all right now until you
reach the Establishment"—The Establishment!—
"since it's clear going and a safe run.

"A happy wedding, a comfortable honeymoon,
certainly not one in a cabin behind the wheel of a
truck looking at star shadows"—star shadows!—"and
then in due time the patter of little feet—two, not
four like Harriet's."

Really, he *was* a savage!

But at the end there crept in a different note,
cryptic yet somehow reassuring . . . that is if she had
needed reassuring.

"If the gem should ever leave its box, call up the
Territorian."

"The fellow is quite mad," said Gemma, and began
munching toast.

When she came down to the garages she found that
the yard man had put a length of waterproof in the

back seat of her car and some old blankets.

"She should be quite comfortable," he told Gemma, "and anyway, you haven't all that far to go now. The Mannerings', isn't it?"

"No, I'm going first to the Rudhill Scientific Block." The Territorian must have been talking with the yard man about her; Gemma had a feeling that everything would be aired and discussed up here.

"Well, that's nearer still," nodded the man, "it's the first of the two turn-offs after Come Again. Goodbye, miss. Goodbye, little girl."

Harriet looked blankly at him, looked just as blankly at Gemma, and Gemma set off.

One mile out of The Alice, the country took over again, only now with a subtle difference. Instead of only showing the finer sides of the Wet in resultant green grass, thicker foliage and new springing trees, several lakes, prompted no doubt by the rains, began to appear, quite a few creeks. Then, without warning, the Lucy River, that was usually only a trickle, came flowing strongly, reaching at some places, it was said, a width of forty miles.

With a girth like that it looked more like an inland sea than a swollen river, and many people were already calling it an inland sea. Only it wasn't, it was the same Lucy River, and in a few years it could be back to its trickle again, even not there at all.

Fortunately the road, even after the river's sudden rise, ran safely and well identified beside the new stretch of water. But if the Lucy had grown any bigger, Gemma thought, it would have enveloped it entirely, a new road would have had to be built. But the dark blue tar had escaped such a fate, and the only effect had been to make it quite a scenic drive, particularly so when you realized where you were, and that was north of the centre of a vast continent, where there had been no rivers, only trickles, and no seas and no lakes . . . until now.

But *now* . . . now it was all changed, and instinctively Gemma halted the car. It was unbelievable, she thought.

There had always been colour to spare in this centre, but it had been from sun on rocks turning them into slabs of violet, or from the heat haze like blue smoke on the ochre horizon, but now the colour came from previously unknown flowers, as far as the eye could see everything, apart from the rippling blue stretch of river, sea or lake, whatever you wished to call it, was pulsing with scarlet, orange and magenta petals.

Gemma caught her breath, then let it go sharply. Here in this once arid waste, this waterless place, actually stood an ibis. Tall, motionless, looking as if it was sculptured out of shining wood, it stared back at her. And not just an ibis but other water birds. Instead of the previous hawks and harriers and a few ground birds there were swans, there were pelicans. There were gulls. In this once-desert, hundreds of miles from any coast, there were gulls.

There were tears in Gemma's eyes as she started off again, a lump in her throat.

The Rudhill Scientific Block proved clearly marked, and in the afternoon after Come Again, which was nothing, and to which, as far as anyone knew, no one had ever come, Gemma left the tar.

As it was not a missiles station, not entailing anything secret or nationalistic, only scientific and exploratory research, there were no guards to pass at the front gate.

Gemma began the long drive to the block.

It was a narrow track, un-tarred, and very little different from the day when it had been laid down. At several spots twigs brushed the car window, rousing the reclining Harriet and sending her plum eyes wide open. But only for seconds; in a few moments she was sleeping again.

Gemma had no fears as to Harriet's reception. She knew the dear Brains, as she called them. They were amiable almost to a bovine state themselves; everything to do with the outer world found them amicably abstracted. It was only when they dealt with their own particular thing, be it mica, wolfram, cosmic rays, permian rock, that they seemed to come really alive. No, they would just pat Harriet on the head, promptly forget her, then return to their respective worlds. They were dears, every one of them, she had no fears about them ... but what, later, about the Mannerings?

She did not know why that thought occurred to her, and she tried to shame herself for even thinking it. Of course the Mannerings would not object to Harriet, they were used to Harrys and Harriets, it was their world. They might make the remark, as Tim Torrance had made about cake, that taking a calf north was like taking coals to Newcastle, but they would never object. Harriet could stop there with Godfather until after the wedding, then, when she had established herself in the Establishment ... now she was saying it! ... she would come down to visit

Godfather and when she left again take Harriet with her.

As though sensing she was in Gemma's thoughts, Harriet sat up now and looked out. There was still nothing to see, but they were climbing a slight hill, and down in the slight valley under the hill the block had been built. It comprised an office, a community dining room, then a number of small, self-contained chalets. Gemma knew all this because she had been here before; she had flown up with Godfather when he had first taken up his post here, flown home again. His chalet was the last of all, which would be advantageous for Harriet. Gemma did not think she would cause any trouble, but if she did feel like kicking up her heels, the remainder of the valley was hers.

She saw the first building loom in sight. No one around as usual. There never was in a scientific place. Scientists did not have time to fill in or to watch out for visitors, nor did they particularly wish to. Their lives were more than occupied. She knew she should call in at the office and present herself first, but she decided to delay that. Better to settle Harriet at once, and anyway, she could not wait to see Godfather. Dear, vague Godfather, who had sent her a letter through Bruce to look up a prescription and bring it along with her, knowing it would take her all that time to sort through his chaos. Dear Bernard, how surprised he would be when he learned how that request to Bruce Mannering had borne fruit.

Gemma lowered the car's speed and was quietly passing the office when someone stepped out of it. It was Mr. Fortescue, she recognized, a valued retainer who understood the vague ways of Brains, and who knew, among other things, that as often as not, if unprompted, then scientists forgot even to eat or sleep. She waved to him.

But Mr. Fortescue did not wave back, he beckoned her. When Gemma did not obey, he stepped in front of the car, which was barely moving now, and called: "Can I see you first, my dear?"

"But I really can't wait, Mr. Forty . . . you see, I have a passenger." Gemma pointed to Harriet and smiled, but the smile old Forty gave back was only fleeting.

"Please, my dear, come into my office first."

Gemma drew up the car, wound up the windows. She did not want Harriet getting out and eating any of the flowers that Mr. Fortescue had very laboriously raised. But then it was goats who ate flowers, wasn't it, not calves. She wondered uneasily why she was being so vague all at once, and decided it was Forty. He had something to tell her. She could sense it. Would he hint, as she suspected must happen some time, that at Godfather's age Godfather shouldn't be out here in the middle of nowhere in case he should be taken ill, gravely ill. But that would be the end of Godfather. Godfather was the kind to die with his boots on.

. . . And that, in Mr. Fortescue's small office, was what Gemma was told a few minutes after.

"He never came in for dinner last night . . . well, we never worried, you know how these brainy men are . . . then no meal again this morning. So I went down. And there he was. A bit of rock in his hand and his head bowed over it, spectacles still on as though he was examining the piece, but not with us

43

any more. You could say he died with his boots on, my dear."

For a long time Gemma just sat there, and old Forty sat with her. Then he went out and came back with tea.

"It's the way he would have wanted to go," he said gently to Gemma, "and the place, too. He only said to me a week ago that of all his journeys into science, this journey had been the best. He loved the centre most of all, and that's why . . ." Old Forty looked significantly at Gemma.

"Yes, Mr. Fortescue?"

"That's why he told me to keep him here. Are you following me, Gemma? Do you know what I'm trying to say?"

"Yes, Mr. Fortescue," said Gemma.

"He said: 'I can't think of any better journey's end than right here. If anything happens, Forty, will you tell my goddaughter?'"

"So you're telling me," she whispered.

"Yes, my dear. He didn't want to be taken back to Sydney, he wanted to stay in the red country that he had come to love so much."

"When—when did he die?" She had been told, but somehow she could not think straight.

"Yesterday."

"Yesterday I was on the road. If I'd been a day before . . ."

"Yes, dear, there are many ifs in life," soothed Mr. Fortescue.

"Where is he?" she asked.

Mr. Fortescue nodded to a little outbuilding, and Gemma bit her lip and nodded back.

"Can I see him? Say goodbye?"

"Yes, dear."

"And then what?" she asked.

"Then we have our outback minister who calls here at times and who has now been contacted. The Reverend Bill . . . he's the Reverend William Flett really . . . always says it's a travesty talking to scientific blokes, that they have all the answers. But the Reverend Bill also says they have good hearts."

"Godfather had a good heart," she said wistfully.

"We all know that. We all loved him. Then shall we say tomorrow? There's a little cleft in the rocks down the incline where he often used to go to rest and think." Mr. Fortescue looked anxiously at Gemma.

"Yes," Gemma said.

He gave her a key and she went sadly across to the building. But all her sadness dropped away as she looked at Godfather. He seemed to be smiling.

"I think," Gemma said lovingly to him, "you found your best rock occurrence yet, Godfather."

She came out again and Mr. Fortescue was waiting for her.

"We can fix you a room up here if you would sooner, my dear. You may feel lonely and deserted down there."

"No, I'd sooner have Godfather's chalet. Besides, I'll have his things to go through."

"You're a wonderful girl, but then he always said that. Please stay on with us as long as you can. The boys, even though they're blind as bats, unaware scientists, like a pretty face about the place. You'd be doing us a service."

"I'd like to stop for ever. I love out here. But I

would only have been here briefly, anyway, only until I married."

"Married? You're marrying up here?"

"To a Mannering. Bruce Mannering," she told him.

"Yes, I know Mannering Park. They've made several complaints."

"Complaints?" Gemma queried.

"It's inevitable with geologists. Our g's try to avoid it, and we do pay compensation, but it sometimes happens like that."

"What happens like that?"

"When geos and mica and wolfram men go out scouting, holes sometimes are left."

"Which turn into water supplies and should please the Mannerings . . . I mean the pastoralists."

"Sometimes," said Mr. Fortescue sadly, "a hole breaks a beast's leg. But we do our best not to let that happen, of course, and we do pay compensation." A contemplative pause. "So you're marrying into the Mannerings."

"Yes."

"Then would you like to contact them, my dear?"

"Oh, no, they don't expect me. I told Bruce I would be married from the barracks and would not be ready for a little while yet."

"I didn't mean quite that. I meant would you like their comfort in your sorrow? Their presence? Mr. Bruce's presence?"

"No," Gemma answered, and she surprised herself. She did not want Bruce, not now! Why didn't she want him? In love you wanted comfort as well as joy. In death you wanted the touch of a hand even more than in life. Yet she didn't want Bruce.

"Then someone else? I feel you should have some-one," persisted Mr. Fortescue. "Have you met anyone up here, my dear?"

"No . . . only a road train man. A Mr. Torrance." Now why had she answered that?

"The Territorian? We all know Tim." Mr. Fortescue smiled warmly. "I think he would come, any-way," he said, "he was very friendly with Bernard."

It was only when she had gone down to the chalet that Gemma realized what she had done when she had mentioned Tim Torrance to Mr. Fortescue. She had established the Territorian and displaced Bruce, and it was Bruce she really wanted. Wasn't it? How-ever, Mr. Fortescue had said that the Territorian would have come, anyway, that is if he was here. But he wouldn't be here. He would be swinging down The Bitumen, boss of the road, stopping every fifty miles to get the fallen beasts on their feet again. At night he would be sleeping in the compartment behind the wheel, and looking through the window at star shadows.

Gemma settled in Harriet, went up to the mess for a meal with the men and was fussed over and petted, then came back and went to bed.

But before she put out the light she stood a moment at the open door. The air was incredibly soft and warm; centre nights were usually like that. The stars seemed as big as gourds, which made it only natural that they cast shadows on the red earth outside the chalet door.

Was the Territorian looking at shadows, too, she thought? Then . . . and a little guiltily:

Was Bruce?

The Reverend Bill Flett arrived the next morning and he sat with Gemma and talked about the centre. As a centre man himself he was glad that Godfather was stopping in the red country. He deserved that, the Reverend Bill told Gemma, he was the finest of all rock himself.

"Yet you're known to say that the scientific men have all the answers," smiled Gemma wanly.

"I do say that, but do you know what? They're the right answers, only put in different terms. They're my answers, His answers, only in scientific language."

Gemma spoke of her forthcoming marriage. She felt she would have liked the Reverend Bill to have solemnized it.

"The Mannerings," he said doubtfully.

"Yes."

"I rather think they might fly up some social dog-collar from Sydney."

"But I would like you."

The Reverend Bill seemed about to say something, then evidently changed his mind.

At noon all the block went down to the resting place that had been prepared, the little cleft where Godfather had often sat and contemplated.

The Reverend Bill chose Psalm Eighteen. The Lord is my rock, my strength and my deliverer ... my buckler, and the horn of my salvation ... my high tower.

My high tower.

The words touched, then gently enclosed Gemma. Tears stopped blurring her eyes and she found she could look up.

She saw the Territorian standing at the back of the others, and as well as comfort from the words that had been spoken she was aware of another comfort. My high tower, she thought. Tim Torrance towered above the others and as he looked across at her she felt a calm and an acceptance that had been denied her before, so he in his way was a high tower as well.

Mr. Fortescue came across and put his arm around her and they all went back to the barracks. There was a big pot of tea and a big slab of project cake, yellow, sawdusty and containing one raisin.

All the Brains came and kissed Gemma, and urged her to stay on. To stay on, anyway, they added, until she left to be married. There was no reason, they pointed out, why she shouldn't keep to the plans she had told them about, and be married from the barracks.

Gemma said she would think it over, then turned to find the Territorian by her side.

"I'm sorry," he said quietly, "for myself as well as for you. Bernard Drews, I mean. I knew him very well and I'll miss him. I have a deep feeling for all these fellows, they're doing work I wish I could have done, but I didn't have those kind of brains, but rock I admired most of all. I've always loved rock. Yes, he'll be a loss. I never dreamed he belonged to you."

"We belonged to each other," Gemma said.

"I can see that now. Why didn't you tell me?"

"Tell you what?"

"That you were coming here."

"Why should I? I mean, we were only passing by."

49

"But we weren't, were we? We met up again. But I'm sorry it had to be like this. What are your plans now?"

"The men want me to stay . . . well, until I leave to be married. I'll think about it, as I said." She paused. "I'm still kind of hollow and unsure."

"Of course you are. That's where your man comes in."

"My man?" She looked at him a little stupidly.

"Your fiancé." He was staring very hard at her, very alertly, not at all stupidly. "That's what fiancés are for. For comfort. For a hand in yours. Don't tell me" . . . his eyes boring now . . . "he doesn't know yet."

"Everyone knows everything up here. You told me that yourself." Her voice had risen a note.

'They hear eventually, yes, but good grief, girl, in a thing like this you don't let them hear, you tell them. Haven't you told Mannering?"

"No. You see, he wasn't expecting me, I mean not yet. I mean, the arrangements were . . . Oh, dear!" Gemma looked distressed, she clenched and unclenched her hands. "Should I have done so?" she implored.

He was silent for quite a long time. Then:

"Not unless you felt you should," the Territorian answered, and he spoke quietly.

"All the same," he went on, "as you're the Future Mrs. Mannering I'd give it a second thought." Another pause, shorter this time, and after it another theme.

"You got my note?"

"Yes."

"In it I told the gem if she ever left her velvet box to call me up, but now I'll say it with more dignity."

"Yes?"

"It's this: If you should need me I'll be waiting, Gemma."

"Why should I need you?" she asked curiously.

"I said if," he reminded her.

"I won't need you."

"Then good for you, but not so good for me. However, what I've said still stands. And remember the high tower."

My rock, my strength, my deliverer, my buckler, my horn of salvation. My high tower.

Gemma was thinking this as she carried down a bottle of milk later to poddy-feed Harriet. Well, the fellow was tall enough, but he was ... and would be ... no tower. Bruce was her tower, and tomorrow she would go on to Mannering Park and begin her new life. She had decided on that.

"You, too," she promised Harriet, "but" ... crumpling for a moment ... "I do wish, darling, you'd been able to meet Godfather."

Harriet just sucked on oblivious, and laughing a little Gemma continued dunking her fingers in milk then inserting them in the calf's sweet pink velvet mouth.

The next day Gemma put Harriet in the back seat again, kissed all the men goodbye, promised the geologists a better deal once she belonged to the House of Mannering and they left holes behind them, then drove out of the block and once more headed north.

CHAPTER FOUR

IT was only some hundred kilometres to the next turn-off, which was Mannering Park. The first turn-off from Come Again had been Rudhill, and because there were no branching roads prior to it, none in the distance as far as Gemma could see, she wheeled with confidence into the much smaller but still sealed way when it occurred an hour later. Twenty minutes later again the road lost its tar, grew narrower and branched a second time, but at that precise moment Harriet set up a moo of protest from the back seat, either for sustenance or exercise . . . Gemma decided to give her both . . . and by the time Gemma had halted the car she was past the branch and the sign with the *two* arrows, one to Mannering Park and one to a place called Boothagullagulla.

When she set off again, Harriet having been duly finger-dunked and duly skipped, Gemma was unknowingly on the way to Boothagullagulla.

It was a charming track, and she found her spirits rising. There were a few gurgling streams, legacies from the Wet, and a few large puddles of leftover water with pelicans sailing on them. There was also a sense of sea, somehow. Gemma even stopped the car to sniff and to listen. It was ridiculous, she knew that, but there was still that sensation of blue water.

She drove on.

Half an hour later . . . how very large were these

properties . . . Gemma knew she was coming to something. She went through a first gate, taking care not to commit that cardinal sin and not shut it carefully behind her, a second gate, a third gate, and was wondering whether one could ever train a calf to perform these little tasks when the homestead surprised her. Delightfully surprised her. It was a typical Australian one-level sprawling building with a colonial encircling verandah like the wide brim round a college hat.

Gemma loved it at once.

She loved it even more as she pulled up. The shallow stairs to the front brim of the hat were wide and inviting and on each rise was a tub of scarlet geranium. There were deep comfortable chairs waiting, and from one of them rose a barely middle-aged man, a man with greying hair and matching, very friendly grey eyes. He threw down the paper he had been reading and at once came down the steps to greet her. Before Gemma could do so, he opened the car door, then extended his hand to help her out. He raised his brows at Harriet, but he did not seem at all put out.

"Hullo, girl," he said to the calf, then he turned and included Gemma. "Hullo, both girls. Welcome to Boothagullagulla."

"Bootha— where?" asked Gemma in dismay.

"It is rather a mouthful, isn't it? Aboriginal, of course."

"Bootha—"

"Gullagulla. Boothagullagulla. And, as I'll show you presently, Miss? Mrs.?—"

"Miss Glasson."

"As I'll show you presently, Miss Glasson, very apt."

"Boothagullagulla?" she queried. "But—but aren't I at Mannering Park?"

"Mannering Park belongs to the Mannerings. I'm Christopher Mitchell. Chris." The pleasant, barely middle-aged man looked expectantly at Gemma, and Gemma told him her first name. He was the kind of man, she knew instinctively, with whom you would want to be on first-name terms at once.

All the same she added pleadingly: "But where is Mannering Park?"

"Mannering Park lies over there." Chris pointed. "A long way over there. We, the Establishment and I, share the same boundary fence and the same track in from The Bitumen. Only, and I think this is where you made your mistake, another twenty miles from the highway there's a fork, and you forked to here instead of to there. I'll have to check up on the finger-post. I haven't been down there for months. Perhaps it's overgrown or even blown down. Or even faded out from our rains. Did you hear about our rains?"

"Yes," said Gemma.

"They were unprecedented, but" . . . knowledgeably . . . "there are more yet to come."

"You think so?"

"I'm sure of it. I make a study of our weather, a close and detailed study, and all the warnings are there."

"You just said the Establishment," slipped in Gemma. "You meant the Mannerings, I take it."

"Forgive my prattling tongue, please, I was just being a fool." He smiled charmingly at her.

"And yet I've heard such foolish talk before," Gemma returned.

54

"Then take no heed. We're all of us up here called something or other. Probably I'm Crazy Chris or Mad Mitchell." He smiled again at Gemma, then called into the house: "How is that teapot, Ludy?"

An aboriginal woman came down the wide front hall. Already she was laden with a tray bearing a pot, cups and a plate of scones.

"I beat you to it, Mr. Chris," she said triumphantly. "I saw the car coming along the track and I said to myself 'This means tea or my name's not Ludy'."

"Your name is Special Ludy, Number One Housekeeper," praised Chris. "Leave it, Ludy, I'll pour."

But Gemma did the pouring. She took over the rites, and as she did so, she felt his eyes on her, particularly pleasant eyes, she thought, very friendly, very kind, and just now very watchful.

"What is it, Chris?" she inquired after a while, finding the steady look a little disconcerting.

"Sorry, Gemma, but you reminded me of someone."

"Someone nice?"

"The nicest."

"You said reminded, then isn't she—don't you see her now?"

"My wife Neroli died in our first year of marriage."

"Oh—I'm sorry."

"It's a long time ago now," he said.

"But still—I mean—"

"Yes. Still that." He nodded at Gemma, understanding what she had not said. There was a little silence.

"Do you live here alone?" asked Gemma presently. "I mean, apart from Ludy and the other employees?"

"My sister Isabel lives with me, only Isabel isn't here just now. Isabel is my twin, unmarried and a wonderful person. *When I see her.*" The last with feeling.

"Is she away a lot?"

"Isabel works like a beaver—no, not for herself, for others. She loves the aboriginal people and they love her. Just now she's out on the Janana Mission while I rough it here."

"I can well imagine that roughing," laughed Gemma, biting into a feathery scone.

Chris Mitchell called to one of his stockmen who was passing to take Harriet out of the car, then let her roam. When Gemma warned that Harriet might eat his lawn, he said good, he had never been over-fond of the mower.

"You're a really very tolerant person," Gemma praised. "A very welcoming one." Then she said impulsively: "I wonder if—"

"If?"

"If the Establishment will be as tolerant and welcoming." She looked directly at Chris Mitchell.

"Look, I told you I was only being a fool when I said what I did," he proffered anxiously.

"Yet Establishment has been said to me before. Several times before. Why are the Mannerings called an Establishment?"

"An establishment means a fixed state, and I guess that's the Mannerings. Well, why not? Permanency is a very good thing."

"And a very rigid thing?"

Chris did not answer. He pretended to be busy drinking. Gemma knew it was pretence because she

56

had had her hand on the teapot before he began, since his cup, she had noticed, was empty.

"I'm sure," he said presently . . . and over-optimistically, or so Gemma construed it . . . "that your calf will be most welcome."

"Chris, do you always tell lies?" Gemma, more relaxed with this man than she could remember being relaxed with any man, laughed it back at him, and refilled his cup.

"We-ell," he avoided. He looked curiously at the calf and then back at Gemma. "Anyway, why *did* you bring her?" he inquired.

"There was nowhere else to take her, and I couldn't abandon her."

"No, you couldn't do that. But why did you fetch her in the first place?"

"But I didn't. She was thrust on me. I certainly didn't start off with her, not from Sydney."

"Sydney?"

"That's where I've come from."

"Thrust, you said."

"Thrust. By a road train boss. A blessed event had occurred, and if he had left the calf among the beasts—"

"Yes, that sometimes happens," Chris nodded. "So you played mother. That was kind of you."

"I didn't feel kind at first, I was infuriated. You see, not only was Harriet thrust at me, she was thrust on—well, on a cake."

"A cake? No, you wouldn't be happy about that."

"Worse was to follow." There was something about this Chris, Gemma thought, that was quite irresistible, you simply had to confide in him. "Harriet was thrust

57

next on to a dress," she went on.

"Dress?" he questioned.

"I had this dress in the back seat. It was a special dress. A wedding dress."

"And the cake, was it——?"

"Yes, it was a wedding cake."

"You were taking this cake and dress to someone up here?"

"No. They were mine," Gemma admitted ruefully.

"Yours?"

"Yes."

Chris nodded, clicked his tongue in sympathy and was thoughtful a while. "And when you came to Boothagullagulla you were really intending to go to the Estab—to the Mannerings?"

"Yes."

"Then you must be Bruce Mannering's bride-to-be."

Future Mrs. Mannering. That was how Tim Torrance had put it. However, Gemma just answered Chris quietly: "Yes."

"Mrs. Mannering." Chris was looking at her very hard, but as soon as he saw her looking back at his hard look, he changed his focus.

"Well now," he said.

A little uneasily Gemma related how Harriet had torn the veil and the gown, but for all that had been forgiven, then finally loved.

"That's a good finality," Chris approved.

"I took her on to the Rudhill block ... do you know the scientific station?"

"I have friends there. I've often run down just for a natter. Up here an hour of intelligent conversation can often do more for a man than a bumper season. Strange, though, you speaking of Rudhill. I've just learned through our grapevine that one of my best friends at Rudhill died this week."

"Bernard Drews," nodded Gemma. She bit her lip to steady it. "He was my godfather." She had hardly said it than she felt his big hand over hers, tight and comforting.

"Steady," he said.

When he saw that Gemma *was* steady, he went on: "So you were old Bernie's girl."

"Goddaughter."

"He must have been proud of you."

"I know I was proud of him. We were terribly close. And to think I just missed him . . ."

"Well, it happens, doesn't it, but nothing happens to the memories. So you went out to Rudhill?"

"The funeral was the next day. After that—well, I came on here, even though the men wanted me to stay on. I could have stayed, too, I wasn't expected at Mannering Park yet. You see, the arrangement was that I was to be married from Rudhill, but with Godfather gone . . ." Gemma sighed.

"I understand." Chris came in gently with it, and Gemma had a warm feeling that he did.

After a while he frowned and touched her hand again. "I should have been there, Gemma. The men are good, but you should have had someone of your own, or at least someone else."

"I did. Well—in a way. He was a friend of Godfather's, too. He was on the road, but he was contacted, and he came."

"I'm glad of that, it must have comforted you."

The high tower, Gemma thought. Aloud she said:

"Yes, it did."

"But he didn't come on here with you?"

"He couldn't. He was on the road, as I said."

"We're all of us on the road once we get going with wheels under us."

"Thirty-six wheels?" Gemma asked Chris.

"Thirty-six ... A road train?"

"Yes."

"And the road boss came back for the service?"

"Yes."

"Don't tell me." Chris was holding up his hand to prevent Gemma. "It wouldn't be Bagsworth or Maloney, they'd never stop, they like their pound of flesh."

"It was Territorian Transport."

"Yes, Tim Torrance's bunch would do just that."

"Only it wasn't the bunch, it was—him."

"Him?"

"Tim Torrance," Gemma said.

"But Tim is the big boss, the boss of the bosses."

"He still keeps in touch," she explained.

"I know that."

"He was driving that day," Gemma told him.

"The day of the blessed event?"

"Yes."

"A blessed event, too, I'd say for Tim." The kind eyes now were frankly admiring Gemma.

"Chris, I am the future Mrs. Mannering," Gemma said sternly.

"Of course," Chris agreed. There was a short silence.

Gemma broke it.

"So you know Tim—Mr. Torrance—the

Territorian?"

"Since the year dot. He used to overland for me before overlanding was done mechanically, and he used to do the impossible, get the beasts through without a loss. He's doing the impossible still, but in the new road train way instead of from a horse. That" . . . proudly . . . "is our Territorian."

"He's been lucky," Gemma said stiffly.

"Not Tim. Farsighted, yes, shrewd, discerning, but the rest has been sheer hard work. Still, it's paid off. He's right at the top now, can thumb his nose at any of the pastoralists, and that's why . . ." But Chris did not finish that.

"Does he thumb his nose at you?" Gemma asked.

"Not Tim. We're old friends. He even gives me cut rates."

"That," said Gemma, "should give you an advantage over the Mannerings."

"The Mannerings," Chris answered briefly, "don't truck with Tim."

He was quiet a while, and then he laughed to himself. "So it was Tim's blessed event," he mused again.

"Yes."

"Then that would make the calf probably my property. Tim was road training the beasts for me."

"Yes, he said Harriet was rightly the property of the pastoralist whose beasts he was carrying, but he also said he didn't always write it down."

"I'll book him for that! No" . . . at an alarmed look in Gemma's face . . . "I'm only joking. Tim is the straightest bloke in the business."

"But the calf . . . but Harriet is still yours, Chris."

"No, yours, Gemma. I don't want her. But—"

"But?"

"But I'll take her later on if you ask me."

"You mean when I go to the Mannerings'?"

"Yes."

"Why should I ask you?"

"Because . . . well . . . that is . . ." A pause. "Look here, take no notice of my babbling. It's high time Isabel got back. I've only Ludy to talk to, and I'm beginning to lose the knack. I say mad things. Mad Mitchell, that's me all right. Now where were we up to?"

"Harriet . . . and if she's not wanted."

"I never said that."

"No, but you didn't say she'd be wanted, either."

They looked at each other, grinned, and knew they were at a deadlock. Gemma tried to break him down, but Chris resisted. In the end he won, and the subject was closed.

Cunningly, successfully, he steered the conversation away from Harriet and her welcome, or lack of it, and began talking instead about Boothagullagulla.

Meaning seagulls.

"Curious how a name, or close to it, can be repeated through time," Chris said. "Boothagullagulla is from the Western Australian dialect, and it was used before white man ever set foot here."

"Boothagullagulla was actually the name of this place?" Gemma asked incredulously.

"Yes," said Chris. "I've established that, or rather Isabel, who is an expert on such things, has. It was always called Gulls."

"But how? We're in the centre of the inland, away

from sea, away from water. Oh, I know I saw sea birds as I came up beside the swollen Lucy River, but they had a reason, even if I could scarcely believe they'd flown this far into the interior. But there's no river here, is there?"

"No," said Chris, "and yet again yes."

"Yes?"

"Ever heard of upside-down creeks?"

Gemma said that she had.

"There are quite a few out here. Sandy river beds, quite often dried up almost to erosion, but underneath there is water. We feel, Isobel and I, that Boothagullagulla was once a waterway, back in the Dreamtime it would be, but through the centuries of centuries strange things have happened, strange things have always happened to this strange country, and the water went down and the sand and the earth came on top. Sort of reversal, if you follow me."

"I do, and I have heard of it, but would it be only here in this particular district, Chris? Only at Boothagullagulla?"

"Yes. When you go to Mannering Park you'll see you're higher and on entirely different kind of ground."

"I know," came in Gemma eagerly, "no sense of the sea as there is here."

"So you felt that, too?"

"Strongly."

"When we go back to the turn-off . . . yes, I'll show you where to change tracks this time . . . we'll detour a little and you can see our lagoon. There's no obvious reason for a lagoon, yet a lagoon is still there."

"With gulls?"

"Gulls," Chris said. "Also whenever your god-father's geo mates came up here exploring and sank a hole, the hole would be filled in a flash."

"So you aren't annoyed like some of the pastoralists?" Gemma asked.

"Never yet seen a beast break its leg on water," Chris returned. "Ready to move now, Gemma?"

"Yes." But Gemma said it a little unwillingly. She could have listened to Chris all day.

While one of the stockmen brought round Chris's car, Chris told Gemma the aboriginal version of Boothagullagulla.

Years ago in the Dreamtime a great snake lived here, and every day he cooled himself from the burning heat in the great water that was also present. But one day a great bird swooped down on the great snake, whereupon the great snake went under the ground, taking with him his cooling water. He intended to remain there until the bird had gone and it was safe for him to come up. Some of the cooling water he left behind in his hurry to escape the bird, and that water had spread and become today's lagoon.

"Ludy told me that," Chris said, "and laughed as she related it. But I'm not sure if she didn't really believe it deep down. Now you follow me, Gemma. First to the lagoon, then to the Mannering turn-off."

It was not far to the lagoon, and Gemma drew up her car beside Chris's and looked in wonder at pastel blue, faintly silver-tinged water, with insects weaving gauzy patterns over it, frogs singing in a busy chorus. It was not deep, in places only measuring several inches, but it was very wide and very strange, even mysterious.

She turned back to the car.

Now she followed Chris along the track she had taken over an hour ago . . . there had followed perhaps the most pleasant interlude she could remember, she thought . . . and at the signboard he drew up and showed her an arrow to Mannering Park and another arrow to Boothagullagulla.

"I must have been dreaming," she admitted.

"It's Dreamtime country up here. Well, best of luck, girl, and don't forget the welcome on the mat for Harriet."

"And me?" Gemma smiled.

"Oh, yes, for you." He said it warmly, sincerely. He waited till she turned into the right fork, waited until she went down the other track, then turned a bend and was out of sight.

For a while the pleasure of Chris Mitchell's company remained with Gemma and made her feel light-hearted. Then slowly, insidiously, something else crept in. Even the scenery took on a different aspect, it seemed to crowd her, to enclose her. I'm being silly, Gemma tried to tell herself, I'm being unfair. It's just that I'm tired, I expect.

Whether Harriet was tired, too, Gemma could not tell, but the calf was distinctly restless. When Gemma came to the first of the gates, she began to moo.

A second gate was passed, a third, fourth, fifth . . . this property appeared to be much larger than Boothagullagulla.

Then Mannering Park began to take shape, and Gemma could see that it was quite expansive, that as well as a number of bungalows, all with barns and sheds and outhouses, there was a private airstrip.

The bungalows were set well apart, Bruce had assured her of that, but because the land was dead level, you still could see each of the houses quite plainly, from the first villa to the last, and there were four of them.

Which one? Gemma thought uneasily. To which one do I go? After the friendliness that had seemed to reach out at her from Chris Mitchell's, she felt like going to none of them at all. For . . . and again she told herself she was being unfair . . . no friendliness seemed to reach out here, in fact—

But she had to stop somewhere, knock somewhere, present herself somewhere, and it might as well be this first place, a timber house with a verandah, not all that unlike Chris's, and yet . . . and yet as different as it possibly could be.

Gemma could not have explained it, explained herself, she could not have put a finger on it, but every step up to the verandah was an ordeal, the ringing of the bell she found on the door a torment. Suddenly all she wanted to do was turn and run, run anywhere before it was too late. Abandon hope, all ye who enter here . . . how ridiculous, Gemma said to herself, can one get?

But she still would have left, and even had turned to leave, when the door opened, and a woman looked out and smiled.

That kindly smile belonging to Hannah Jason, Mr. Bruce's housekeeper, as Hannah was soon explaining to Gemma, did the trick. It brought Gemma to her senses and into Bruce's home.

Gemma followed Bruce's housekeeper down the long hall.

CHAPTER FIVE

"SO you're Mr. Bruce's young lady." Despite Gemma's protestations that she did not want tea ... more tea ... tea again was being poured.

"I've been wondering what you'd be like. You see, I've been with the Mannerings since Mr. Bruce was born, you could say in a way we arrived at the same time," Hannah laughed. "But I didn't think I'd find out about you for a week yet. Mr. Bruce was not expecting you until then. He knew you'd be getting married from Mannering Park after all and not from Rudhill as you'd planned, not after your godfather's death, but he still thought you wouldn't arrive quite yet."

"He—Bruce knew of Godfather's death?" Gemma said it a little hollowly. He could have come, she thought. He could have got in touch.

"There's very little we don't know up here," said Hannah proudly, "it's like reading a newspaper, the latest is always out by the next day at least, sometimes before that. I think you were very clever to have come straight to Mr. Bruce's house like you did, dear, not knowing it as his place."

"It was the nearest," said Gemma, still a little hollowly. Surely Bruce could have done something, she thought, sent a message, telephoned. Come.

"Not that you can stay, of course," Hannah was saying busily. "Mrs. Mannering wouldn't like that.

You'll be staying at the main house with her until the big day. Oh, dear!"

"What is it?" asked Gemma.

"She's away. Mrs. Mannering and Vida are in Adelaide. It'll have to be Miss Janet, then. I still call her that, though she's not now, of course."

"Where," asked Gemma as steadily as she could, "is Bruce?"

"Up country. In a place like this there's always a lot of up-country and out-country work."

"But he knew I was coming."

"I told you, dear, he didn't expect you yet." Evidently Hannah was thinking romantically that Gemma was concerned about Bruce's return. "Don't worry, it'll be all the nicer when he does get back," she cheered.

. . . Will it? Gemma thought.

She only sipped at the tea and only nibbled at the cake Hannah provided.

"I'm sorry, Hannah, I'm not hungry. I took the wrong turn-off and found myself at Boothagullagulla instead of Mannering Park. Mr. Mitchell gave me tea."

"Mr. Bruce," said Hannah rather unhappily, "won't like that."

"Why?"

"Well, you know how it is with country neighbours, they're not always the best of neighbours."

"I liked Mr. Mitchell," Gemma said firmly.

"I'm sure you did, dear, and I know he'd like you," Hannah said sincerely. "Now go into the lounge and rest, then I'll have one of the men drive you across to Miss Janet's."

"Who is Miss Janet?"

"She's Mr. Bruce's elder sister, Mrs. Willis. Vida is a younger sister, and still unmarried. There were three Mannering children—Janet, Bruce, and Vida. But of course you know all this."

"No," admitted Gemma, "I don't. I didn't know Bruce long before we—"

"Now that's what I call real romantic," beamed Hannah, "it's like in a book. I'm sure Miss Janet will tell you all you should know."

"*If* I was going," said Gemma. "But I'm not." She saw Hannah's startled look and asked rebelliously:

"Why should I?"

"Well, Mrs. Mannering is a—a—"

"A stickler?"

"Yes, dear, that's it. A good woman, dear. Very good. But things always have to be done properly, and after all, it doesn't hurt us to do them that way, does it?"

"It would hurt me right now to go across to another house, Hannah. I'm too tired. I respect Mrs. Mannering's views, and if she were here I certainly would do as she wanted because of her seniority. But seeing Bruce is absent, I know of no reason why I shouldn't stop here, or why I should go to his elder sister."

"No," agreed Hannah, "I suppose that does make sense with Mr. Bruce out of the house the way he is, but you will tell him when he returns, won't you, that it was your idea."

"Of course I will. It is my idea. And now if you'll show me my room I'd really like to rest."

"Certainly, dear, I always keep the bed made up and everything aired. You just take a nap, and later on you can ring Miss Janet and tell her. I mean, I wouldn't like her to think I'd taken it all on myself." For an old employee, Gemma thought, Hannah sounded apprehensive.

"I'll do that," she assured her, and, about to follow the woman, she said:

"Oh, there's Harriet."

"You brought someone else?"

"No need to fuss, Hannah, it's just a very small person." Gemma smiled fondly. "Actually a baby."

"You—have a baby?"

"Yes."

"Mr. Bruce never said . . . I'm sure Mrs. Mannering doesn't know . . ."

"It's a calf. Can it be let out, please?"

Hannah's face cleared, then immediately clouded again. "A calf! I don't know whether Mr. Bruce—"

"Let her roam around." Gemma pushed past the woman into the room that had been indicated, then closed the door. She did it firmly. What was all this? she thought. Where have I come to? What have I put myself in for? Am I dreaming it all? Chris Mitchell said it was a land of Dreamtime.

She went to the window to look out, but found to her chagrin that she couldn't see for foolish tears.

She recalled Chris Mitchell's steadying "Steady", and presently found she could see again.

Not that there was much to look at. The surrounds of the homestead were strictly utilitarian. It was neat enough, concrete had to be neat, Gemma thought, but she longed for a lawn, even an untidy lawn. Lawns made her remember Harriet again. What had happened to Harriet?

She left the room once more.

She could not see Hannah, so she let herself out of the flyscreen door and looked around. There was the usual homestead "shop" with its sledgehammers, crowbars, crosscut saws, scythes and sickles hanging neatly, but somehow the smell she had always loved in her friends' fathers' "shops", that smell of old leather, creosote and sweat seemed less pungent here, though the neatness, she had to admit, was greater. It was the same in the stables. Gemma had always been fascinated with stables. The hooks attached to the walls for brushes and wither pads. The bridles with their buckles ·in their proper places and with the strap ends in their keepers and runners. But most of all the clean sweet air, not the meticulousness. Here, the meticulousness definitely won.

She left the stables and examined the cattle pens, which she found empty. Evidently the cattle were up country or out country, or even recently road trained south. By Bagsworth or Maloney, she added silently, certainly not by the Territorian. Chris had told her that the Mannerings never trucked by the Territorian. Now what, she wondered, had happened there?

About to leave again, she saw a lonely little figure in the furthest pen. Harriet. Harriet looking wistfully back at her.

"Oh, darling," said Gemma, and went up to the calf.

There was certainly no harm the small thing could do to anything outside since everything outside appeared concrete and unable to be damaged. A little angrily, Gemma let out the calf. It kicked up its heels, but not liking the feel of hard cement came back to her.

"Tomorrow I'll take you out to a paddock, Harriet," Gemma promised, "and we'll skip. Meanwhile I'll go and beg some milk."

Hannah was quite agreeable . . . but still, Gemma could see, apprehensive. She had a kind heart, though, and came out with Gemma, and when Gemma grew tired, for feeding the hungry calf was not an easy job, she took over from her. She enjoyed it, too. Gemma could see that.

"I was brought up on a farm," Hannah told Gemma, "not a station. A station's different. You don't get down to earth with things the same as on a farm." She dunked her fingers in the milk then quickly transferred the fingers to Harriet's pink plush mouth. "Only don't say anything to Mr. Bruce," she appealed.

"I won't," promised Gemma. Again she was thinking: What is all this? Am I dreaming it all? Bruce is the dearest of men, the most understanding of men, and I love him.

I love him.

The two women settled Harriet down, then went back to the house. Hannah, now that she had been reassured by Gemma that she would not be blamed for anything, seemed very happy to have Gemma there. Probably, even though country born and bred, sometimes she became a little lonely, eager for her own sex's company. For so far Gemma had not seen any other women around.

She mentioned this, and Hannah said no, that the only women, apart from the Mannering women, were the lubras.

"When the children were very small they had a nursery governess from the city, but as soon as they were old enough they went away to boarding school." Hannah, as she spoke, was beginning to set a place for one in the large dining room, and she was rather ruffled when Gemma stopped her.

"I'm not eating by myself in there," Gemma protested, "I'm coming out to the kitchen with you."

"Oh, no, you couldn't do that."

"Why?"

"It's never been done, that's why. If Mrs. Mannering ever knew—"

"Mrs. Mannering won't know, though what the fuss is about I don't know myself. To my way of thinking it's much more inhospitable to set me in there than to let me share a table here."

"But—"

"Oh, I agree it could be different when the family was about—I mean, Hannah, I'd go along with Mrs. Mannering then even if I didn't actually see eye to eye with her, but to isolate me now would be just too ridiculous, even unkind. Anyway, I'm not going to stay in any dining room. Like it or not, I'm having a corner of your big kitchen table."

"Oh, I like it very much, it's lovely to have someone, only—"

"Then take those things back at once. I'll bring the tray." Gemma picked up the tray and marched to the kitchen, and Hannah, a little uneasily at first, then beginning to enjoy herself, began setting up two places in the kitchen.

There had been an element of strategy as well as community spirit in Gemma's insistence. In this way, she was thinking, I'll hear more of the Mannerings, and more I certainly must hear when within the month I'll be Mrs. Mannering junior.

Future Mrs. Mannering. Again she heard Tim Torrance saying it.

"I met a road train boss coming up," she told Hannah. "A Mr. Torrance."

"The Territorian." Hannah smiled warmly. "He's a wonderful man."

"He told me he didn't truck for the Mannerings."

"No. I think ... only think, mind you ... that Mrs. Mannering didn't approve of the very fast way he came up. I suppose when you've been years and years in a place establishing it, over a century, counting your ancestors, making it what it is, it would be galling to see someone new suddenly get so rich."

"I don't think so, I think I'd be glad for them. I know at least I'd admire their spirit."

"Is this too much, dear?" Hannah broke in rather hurriedly, displaying a piled plate. "Shall I take something off?"

"Nothing. I think I'll even come for seconds."

Hannah beamed, and the meal began.

Gemma did not mention the Territorian again, but she did get back to the Mannerings, and because they probably were the only people now in her life, Hannah was eager to talk.

"Mr. Bruce was the most beautiful baby. I told you we both practically arrived here at the same time. I remember thinking when I saw him that if ever I had a child I would like one just like that. Only" ... a hunch of her shoulders ... "I never married."

"You had the care of Bruce?"

"Always. He went off to college at eight and was there till eighteen, but in between when he was home he was always my responsibility. And he never changed. He was good-looking as a child and he's good-looking now. Don't you agree? But then" . . . archly . . . "of course you would."

"I would regardless," Gemma assured her. "Bruce is a handsome man." She paused. "Tell me about his sisters."

"Janet is barely a year older than her brother. When she was born Mrs. Mannering was naturally very disappointed."

"Naturally disappointed?"

"A man child was wanted, of course. There had to be a Mannering."

"I see. Go on."

"So she wasted no time starting Bruce. It was just as well, I often told myself, he was a boy, otherwise . . ." Hannah gave an apologetic cough and gave her attention to eating for a while.

"Vida came years after. No problem over her since there already was a son. Only a problem now of marriage."

"Is that a problem?" asked Gemma.

"Well, it is in this case. You see, dear, the Mannerings are not just any family, they're—they're—"

"A dynasty?"

"I don't rightly know what you mean by that, but it sounds like what I'm trying to say."

"Is Mr. Mannering alive?"

"He died years ago."

"Yet still Mrs. Mannering holds on to all the trappings."

75

"I don't rightly know what you mean by that, either, but yes, she does like things done as they always were."

"But how would she know? She married into the Mannerings, she wasn't one herself. Why, she might have been a Smith, a Brown, a Jones."

"No, she was a Mannering. The only Mannering. A terrible disappointment to her parents, which probably accounted for her anxiety to have Bruce, a *man* child, herself."

"But I don't understand . . . she was a Miss Mannering, and now she's Mrs. Mannering."

"A deed poll or something of the sort," said Hannah vaguely, "for her husband and herself to keep the name alive."

"An odd husband," Gemma said, but Hannah would not comment on that.

She did, however, say before they closed the subject by mutual consent:

"The Mannerings were here first of all. They pioneered it. The interior wasn't opened up when they came. There were tribes roaming it, there were wild animals, but nothing else at all. It does make you wonder, doesn't it?"

"Yes," said Gemma, but she doubted if she was wondering the same thing as was Hannah, and, if she was, if she was reaching the same conclusion.

She went to bed soon after the evening meal. It had been a long and very amazing day and she found she was tired.

For a while, however, sleep eluded her. Gemma always had had a distinct feeling about houses. She had visited a lot of houses in her school days. When you are a boarder, day girls frequently take pity on you and invite you home. Many homes she had liked at once, felt at ease in at once, but others somehow repelled her.

She could not go as far as to say that Bruce's house repelled her and she certainly liked Hannah very much, but—

But I haven't come *home*, Gemma thought.

She sighed, turned over, and when she opened her eyes again, it was dawn.

Gemma showered, dressed quickly, then went along to the kitchen. Early as she was, Hannah was there before her. But then she had expected that of Hannah. Hannah obviously had not expected Gemma, though, and she looked at her in disbelief, and then she smiled.

"I was just thinking of taking in an early cup."

"Early breakfast will be even better. Breakfast with you." Gemma put enough emphasis on that to discourage Hannah from making any protests.

Hannah began breaking eggs into a pan.

"Didn't the Mannering girls get up early?" Gemma asked later, buttering toast.

"As soon as Mr. Bruce left college, he set up house here. I came to look after him. So you could say, having left the main homestead, I didn't see much of the girls. But as young teenagers, they were not so keen on early rising, I recall, but Mrs. Mannering was strict about that. She wouldn't permit any lay-abouts, as she called it." Hannah added loyally : "And rightly so, too."

"But at times—" Gemma heard herself excusing. Surely the girls hadn't been entirely paragons, she was thinking privately; even the most righteous child occasionally kicks over the parental traces.

Almost as if she spoke aloud, Hannah said:

"Miss Janet was a little inclined to rebel, I recall. There were a few protests. Just as later when she had her eye on— Well, all the girls did, and I don't blame them. But of course, it couldn't be considered."

What couldn't? And whom had Janet had her eye on?

But Gemma would not have dreamed of asking Hannah. Hannah was far too nice to probe. Also, Gemma suspected, already Hannah was feeling a little guilty. She would not want to make her feel worse.

"I'm going out in my car this morning. I'll take a run round Mannering Park." To cheer Hannah, Gemma added, and hated herself for it, for she had no intention of carrying it out: "I might call on Janet."

Hannah, encouraged, said: "There's petrol in the bowser, dear. Lunch will be whenever you get back."

Gemma went down to the barn and released, then led Harriet to the car.

"I'm going to skip you somewhere, Harriet, how do you like that? I can't promise you buttercups to tread on like a nice little cow should tread, but we should find something better than all this cement."

Mannering Park, she decided an hour later, was like a vast showground, or even a small village. There were roads and buildings and settlements everywhere.

One road led towards the master house . . . no, in this instance it would be a mistress house. In spite of Bruce, there was no doubt that Mannering Park was a matriarchy.

Gemma drove near, but not too near. It was the same as Bruce's house, only larger, which it would need to be for a family. Later on when she and Bruce had their family, they would need more rooms than in the satellite cottage, so would they move into the mistress house instead? Make it a master house? After all, Bruce as the only male representative ...

Gemma looked long at the house. She had not fallen in love with Bruce's house, she remembered, but this place ...

She stopped a little shiver of distaste, thanked her lucky stars, as she had thanked them many times before this, that Mrs. Mannering was not yet present, that she at least could grow used to the idea of becoming one of the Establishment, then drove on again.

To the west she saw another villa, probably Janet's. There was a fourth to the north, as yet incomplete. Waiting for Vida?

No wonder, *no wonder* they were the Establishment. An establishment, Chris Mitchell had said, means a fixed state, and this was a very fixed state, she decided.

She found an empty paddock with a satisfactory supply of grass in it. Harriet was plainly delighted. She was just learning to graze.

Gemma sat on the rail and baby-sat. The sun beat pleasantly down on her shoulder blades and the sky was a flawless blue. The horizon was limitless. As far as Gemma could look, east, west, south, north, there was space.

It was quite beautiful, too. The Salvation Jane had intruded in some places ... now why had she said intruded? Yet it must be an intrusion, because the Jane was a weed, and the Mannerings would frown on weeds. Anyway, its unbelievable blue almost shouted at her. Just as well, Gemma thought, there is a shout, or a colour burst, or—or something; the place is too perfect, too ordered, too detached.

A sudden loneliness overtook her. Far to the north she could faintly see a boundary fence. On the other side of the fence would be Chris Mitchell's Boothagullagulla. All at once she wanted quite desperately to drive out to that fence, climb over it, escape.

Instead she collected Harriet and hugged her so hard the little mite mooed and gave Gemma a reproachful look.

She drove back to the homestead in time for another of Hannah's colossal meals. Hannah did not ask her if she had called on Miss Janet, so Gemma did not bring up the subject.

She kept safely to food, and recipes, and how Hannah would have to teach her to cook, then grossly over-indulged by a glowing Hannah, she tottered out to the verandah to sleep the meal off.

Around an hour later she opened her eyes, vaguely conscious of movement somewhere, of something breaking the station quiet.

She sat up and looked out. Across the fields rode a posse of men. Even in the distance her first glance clearly established Bruce. He rode in front, very straight, very efficient, very disciplined. Even after a long drive, for Hannah had said the men had been away for days, he looked impeccable and freshly turned out.

How very handsome he was! Gemma sat gazing at

80

him, admiring the perfect co-ordination of his gear, even though it was only working gear. Browns, fawns, a subtle touch of tan at the throat. How different, how very different, from oil-stained pants and a black sweatshirt. Now why had she thought that?

He was coming nearer, so Gemma got up and waved. He looked over, then raised his whip to her.

But it was some time before he joined her on the verandah. That was only to be expected, of course, he would have to give orders to the men.

But what was not expected was Bruce's casual kiss on Gemma's brow. Gemma could not have said exactly what she had waited for, but she did know that it wasn't that. Nor Bruce's:

"I didn't bank on you coming for some time yet, dear. You must tell me about it. But after my bath first, of course."

"Of course, Bruce." It was on the tip of Gemma's tongue to add: "Though you certainly don't look as though you need a bath. You look as you always look, and that is—"

How *did* Bruce always look? But Gemma asked this only of the verandah post, for Bruce now had gone inside.

How—*how* had Bruce always looked to her?

CHAPTER SIX

WHEN Bruce came out again he was all in cream, the only colour a blue and white polka dot cravat at his throat. He looked cool, relaxed and very much the gentleman of the land. Gemma told him so proudly, her moment of doubt gone, and Bruce frowned slightly and said:

"Yes, but the gentleman is a little concerned. I suppose you know beef is not king any more? Our exports are down. Nothing drastic, of course, but we like to keep a watchful eye on things like that."

"By gentleman I meant *gentleman*, Bruce, not man of means, I meant *you*. You look wonderful."

"Thank you, Gemma. I was really unhappy about not being here to greet you, but as I said, you were not expected yet. Particularly following your sad news."

"I'm glad I didn't know that you'd heard of my news, Bruce, otherwise I would have expected you." If there was a note of reproach in Gemma's voice, it was very faint.

"But, Gemma, up here we learn of everything. I was, as I just said, regretful when I learned of Mr. Drews' death, knowing that you were fond of him."

... Regretful when Bruce learned! Bruce had known Gemma was fond of him!

Regretful ... fond. What pale words were these! Gemma sat very still a moment.

"Also," went on Bruce, blandly unaware of any tension, "there's another reason, Gemma. There's never been any love lost between the scientists and the pastoralists, my dear."

"Some pastoralists." Gemma was thinking of Chris Mitchell.

Bruce raised his brows, but made no comment. "At times," he went on, "there have even been raised voices. In their search for whatever they've been searching for" . . . a slightly acid note . . . "they've been less than considerate."

"I know," nodded Gemma, "holes in the ground to break a beast's leg, yet also holes in the ground for water."

"As you see, we don't need water."

"No, not now, but—" However, Gemma decided not to pursue that.

She did speak on behalf of Godfather, though, she did point out that as a permian rock man only looking for occurrences he had trodden on no toes.

"There are other ways of treading on toes, Gemma," Bruce argued. "Haven't you ever considered who financed Mr. Drews?"

Gemma stared at him in bewilderment What a very odd thing to ask!

"No, you never have," triumphed Bruce. "Then we did. The taxpayer did. And—and do please forgive me, my dear, but it's been quite an imposition."

"Imposition?" she queried.

"Permian rock. Something from the beginning of time. I mean, Gemma, where does that hoo-ha get us? At least the geos might strike oil, even if they make nuisances of themselves doing it, but going back into

83

the past like that—!"

"The Dreamtime," said Gemma. She felt she was dreaming herself.

"Exactly. So now you know why we weren't exactly buddies."

"Some pastoralists were," she pointed out.

"Not the Mannerings."

"You mean the Establishment."

"So you've heard of that." Bruce did not seem at all upset. "We're quite proud of it. After all, we were the first here."

"After the aborigines."

"I wasn't counting them, of course," Bruce said a little sulkily, and Gemma decided that perhaps she had gone too far, though all the same Bruce still had not considered her.

But when he turned and smiled back when she put her hand over his in mute apology, all was well again. How handsome he was, how presentable.

"We must mark our first occasion together at Mannering Park with a toast," he insisted, then he actually reached under the table and brought up a bell. He tinkled the bell.

A bell here in the middle of nowhere! Gemma was not aware she had said that aloud until Bruce corrected:

"You mean at Mannering Park, Gemma. And why not? We're not savages because we're surrounded by a savage country. Surely you don't frown on such little niceties?"

"Of course not." Gemma said it faintly; said, also, that a gin squash, a long one, would be fine, Hannah. Hannah, who had obeyed the summons, nodded and left them again. They both sat back.

Bruce spoke of trivialities until Hannah had brought the tray and left once more. The woman looked a little strained, Gemma thought. Gemma also thought that Bruce had something else to say to her apart from those polite trivialities. There was a firm line to his lips and a slightly austere look.

But at least he waited until he had toasted her.

"Dear Gemma," he said, raising his glass.

"Dear Bruce," said Gemma, raising hers.

They both drank, then looked out on Mannering Park again.

Bruce broke the silence.

"I was a little disturbed when Hannah told me you were staying here, Gemma. I had a few things to say to her."

"To Hannah?"—So that was why the poor woman looked strained.

"Yes. She should have put you right the moment you came here, dear."

"Right?" she questioned.

"Sent you along to my sister Janet's, my mother being away."

"Oh—that." Gemma made a laugh out of it, but it was not easy, for she had a certain feeling that Bruce was not going to laugh back.

She was correct in that feeling. Bruce didn't laugh.

"Yes—that," he said.

"Well, put Hannah right out of your thoughts—and your blame. She did tell me what I should do, but I just told her my own ideas on the subject." Somewhere inside of her Gemma felt like adding: "And that should please you, Bruce, that the future Mrs. Mannering promptly put an employee in her place."

But she didn't say it. Also she could tell that Bruce was very displeased.

"You know my views, Gemma. I told you in Sydney that most certainly you would stay with my mother at the big house before our wedding, never here."

"I answered that I would stay with Godfather," Gemma reminded him, and felt a sharp return of the pain of loss that had been eased in her these last few days.

"I know, dear," Bruce said sympathetically. "And don't think I don't commend you when you left Rudhill as soon as everything was over. I mean, Gemma, one woman among all those men!"

She looked at him in astonishment. Every one of those men was nearing sixty. If a stray here and there had got in, say a young pup of fifty, then his eyes, like the rest of the eyes, never got far from a scientific treatise. Yet Bruce thought . . . could think . . .

"You are," pointed out Bruce, "a very lovely girl."

It was nice to hear, but it was just not good enough. Gemma drank the rest of her gin squash in one reckless gulp and sent Bruce's eyebrows soaring once more, but at once she felt better herself.

"I was tired, Bruce. I wanted to bed down at the first place I came to. Hannah did point out a few things, but I wouldn't listen. Now can't we leave it at that?"

"Certainly, my sweet. After all, no harm is done. And as soon as we've had our drinks . . . I've had my drink . . . I'll get you across to Janet's."

"Your sister's?"

86

"Yes."

"Why?"

"Oh. Gemma, we've gone through all this before," sighed Bruce.

"No, we haven't. That's the trouble—I've settled here. Why can't I stay on?"

"Darling, it wouldn't be correct. I know you come from Sydney, and Sydney isn't really very concerned with such things, but it still isn't the way *we* do things. We're conventional, Gemma. It may sound absurd to you—"

"With a housekeeper in the house, it does."

"But" . . . ignoring her . . . "it's still the way we do things."

A moment's silence. Then :

"Oh, my dearest," said Bruce in a low tone, "don't think it will be always like this. Because we have certain standards now there's no cause for you to believe it won't be wonderful for both of us later on. I can assure you, Gemma, I'm very much the male. As my chosen mate, my love, you'll have no complaints to make over that." It was said suavely, even with a thrilling undertone, a tingling significance, but Gemma—

Gemma felt sick.

"So you will pack your bags, dear?" Bruce asked.

"Yes," she said expressionlessly.

"Meanwhile I'll ring Janet and tell her we'll be coming across. Don't look so crestfallen. We'll have dinner together at Janet's. Then don't forget you're only a short drive away from me, I'm only a short drive from you."

"Yes."

"Now go, Gemma, and fix things up."

"Yes." Gemma rose. She felt that suddenly she had become a zombie. She got as far as the verandah door, then remembered and turned.

"What about Harriet?" she asked.

"What do you mean, Gemma?"

"The calf," she explained.

"I knew you were drinking too fast!" he complained.

"She was given to me, Bruce. She would have been trampled on. Her mother had given birth in a road train."

"You mean she dropped this calf? For goodness' sake, Gemma, don't make a human event out of it!"

"She has seemed that to me," admitted Gemma. "When I wanted something to love when I was lonely, she was there."

"I understand you've brought a calf here." Bruce's voice was cold. "We'll go into that later. In the meantime I'll take you to Janet's."

"But Harriet—"

"I told you, I'll go into that later."

"I can't go without Harriet," she insisted.

"Then we'll get her over tomorrow. Janet mightn't have a suitable position, and you've already found the beast a corner."

"Yes."

"Then tomorrow, Gemma. Now I'll ring Janet." For a brief moment Bruce paused, then actually permitted a smile. "It will be all right," he reassured her, and he kissed her brow again. "Dear, dear Gemma!"

"Dear, dear Bruce," Gemma said mechanically, and followed him down the hall.

It was only when she was putting the few things she had taken out of her case back into the case again that Gemma realized she had not kissed Bruce back. Not once. Perhaps, she thought a little vaguely, I'm not the kissing kind.

Yet when she came to the kitchen to thank Hannah, a hurried thanks since Bruce now was blowing the horn for her to come, Gemma surprised herself—and the housekeeper.

She put her arms round and hugged Hannah, kissed her. They stood for a moment together, then Gemma wiped away a tear and Hannah blew her nose. Then Gemma left the house.

Bruce had the car door open for her, and she could see her bags at the back.

"We'll bring your own car across tomorrow," he said, "also speak about the calf later on."

Before Gemma could answer, he released the brake of his own Mercedes, stepped on the accelerator, then spun across the several miles to the second satellite of the mistress house. To Janet's, the elder sister's, where Gemma was now to stay until the matriarch returned. I mustn't say that, I mustn't think that, Gemma reproved herself. Mrs. Mannering is Bruce's mother, so she will be my mother, too. All will be well.

But with the turning of the wheels, she felt her heart turning. She dared not look in the direction of Boothagullagulla, to Chris Mitchell's, because she knew she would cry out. It will be different, she tried to tell herself, when you meet Janet. Janet is Bruce's sister, and will be your sister soon. You love Bruce, so you'll love Janet.

The Mercedes was pulling up, and a figure was

detaching itself from where it lounged against a verandah post, then coming down the front steps.

Janet. Janet Willis who had been Janet Mannering.
Friend or foe? The eyes, very like Bruce's eyes, looking
back into Gemma's, revealed nothing.

"Welcome and all the usual stuff," Janet Willis said.
She extended a cool cheek to Gemma, then led the
way up to the house again.

"Jim's out at the Rest," Bruce's sister told him as
they all sat in the lounge. It was a very suburban-
looking lounge. Gemma felt it should have taken more
advantage of its unique position. She would have preferred stained floors to carpet, cane to teak, rattan to
damask.

"Then it will be nice for you to have Gemma until
Mother returns," said Bruce.

"Nice," Janet agreed without a flicker either of
enthusiasm or dismay.

"When will Mother get back?" Bruce inquired.

"Quite soon She's doing the engagement and wedding shopping." A quick quirk at Gemma. "You
didn't know, did you, Gemma, that Vida and I are
to be your bridesmaids?"

"No, but it would be what I wanted."

"Thank you," coolly. "I hope, too, you'll approve
of the colours Mamma will choose. And the style. I
hope it compliments yours. What is your style?"

"Was," sighed Gemma.

"Was?"

As briefly as she could, Gemma related the wedding
cake and wedding gown story. After all, they'd have
to learn some time.

Janet's face gave nothing away, but Bruce's gave

away plenty.

"That damned calf will have to go!" he snapped.

"Dear brother, what waste! She would make an excellent veal calf," Janet said slyly.

"No!" broke in Gemma, agitated.

"Take no notice of her, Gemma," Bruce said sharply, "but do take notice of me when I say you can't keep her. The Mannering Park cattle are number one grade. AI, we're labelled. Good heavens, we couldn't take the risk of accepting an interloper. She might have some kind of disease."

"She hasn't. Her mother had been passed as number one grade, AI, whatever it is, as well" ... Gemma supposed she had ... "and before she dropped the calf she was a prize strain."

"How do you know this?" Bruce asked curiously.

"I was there when it happened ... well, very soon after."

"But *how*?" insisted Bruce.

"Harriet was born ... dropped on a road train. The driver thought she could be trampled on. So—so he passed her on to me."

"What colossal nerve! I'll have a word with Bagsworth over this."

"It wasn't Bagsworth," she told him.

"Then Maloney."

"It was the Territorian Transport."

Bruce had risen from his easy chair. He walked to one end of Janet's lounge, then back again.

"I might have known," he said. "That man—"

"Bruce, the *driver* handed Gemma the wretched thing. Don't put everything on to Tim Torrance." It was Janet, and her voice had risen a note. "My

brother" ... Janet now had turned to Gemma ...
"has a thing about Torrance. It all happened last year
when—"

"Janet, shut up!"

"Really, Bruce! In front of your fiancée!"

"I'm glad, anyway, you haven't said in front of your
sister, for by heaven, Janet—"

Janet came in quickly and diplomatically with:
"Are you staying for dinner?"

"No."

"Then go home, Bruce, and cool down. You should
remember that a Mannering never boils over, only
simmers. Come along, Gemma, I'll show you your
room, after which we'll eat together. Jim will be out at
the Rest until Friday, and I think Bruce would benefit
from an early night. Sorry and all that, brother.
Forgive?"

Bruce did not answer.

"Well, forgive, anyway, in front of Gemma," Janet
suggested lightly, but there was a sting somewhere.
Bruce, however, must have decided to go along with
the idea.

"Goodnight, Janet. We'll forget all this. Goodbye,
my dear, it is lovely to have you here."

Bruce crossed to Gemma, gave her her third kiss
today on her brow, then left.

Across the suburban-looking room, Janet gazed at
Gemma, then raised one sardonic brow.

"As you see, we're a very nice family," she said.

Janet did not attempt to show Gemma her room, in
fact she seemed to have forgotten it.

"Bruce will have to take a good hard look at himself," she mumbled, as much to herself as to Gemma. "The old order changeth and all that. We're not quite the kings that we were, not now that beef has dropped. Oh, we're all right. Don't look alarmed, Gemma. Your children will be attending the same exclusive schools as we did. But the winds of change will be creeping in . . . already have crept. For instance where the Mannerings once paled when I mentioned Tim Torrance's name—"

"Bruce didn't pale, he went scarlet."

Janet ignored the interruption. "Where the Mannerings once paled when I mentioned Tim Torrance's name . . . *socially* . . . now I believe our dear parent will lend a sympathetic ear if Vida sings that song."

"What song? Janet, what are you talking about?"

"About Tim Torrance, the Territorian, our local Johnny Come Lately, who, with his trucks and his trains and his big contracts, can now put many more zeros to his millions than the Mannerings ever dreamed of."

"You mean—"

"I mean when I was Vida's age, I, too, had an eye for Tim Torrance. What girl hadn't?" A pause. "Still has. But it was different then, the Territorian was only climbing up the rungs and the Mannerings were at the ladder top. But Tim's at the top himself now, and the Mannerings . . . well . . ." She shrugged.

"You were—attracted to Mr. Torrance?"

"I was crazy about him, but Mamma soon saw to that." A narrowing of Janet's eyes as she added: "As I soon saw to her. But now it's little Vida's turn, and it looks as if she could win. Mannering Park could do with a boost."

"But Mr. Torrance mightn't feel like that about Vida."

"Not about Vida particularly, but certainly about the Establishment," Janet said carelessly, as though it was something to be taken for granted.

"Anyway, that's what the shopping spree *really* is about. Not you, dear, Vida. For the first time in Mannering history someone not a pastoralist, or equal to, is being invited to a Mannering 'do'. The Territorian is. Like it or lump it, Gemma, my dear brother is going to have to shake Tim Torrance's hand when he comes and murmur the expected pleasantries."

"I don't mind," Gemma assured her.

"I didn't mean you, I meant Bruce, and when I said have to, I meant have to. The Territorian can scarcely attend an engagement party and not step forward to offer his congratulations."

"Engagement party?" asked Gemma.

"Yours, dear. Bruce's. It occurs before the wedding. You didn't think I meant Vida's, did you? Not this soon."

"No, I didn't think you meant Vida's, but—"

"But will he come, you're thinking. I don't know." Janet had gone to the window ostensibly to fix the venetian blind, but Gemma saw that her fingers were trembling, and that she barely touched the cords.

She turned back to Gemma.

"Vida is five years younger than Bruce and six years younger than I," she said. "You could say I was born six years too soon. So" . . . a flick of her head to a framed photo on the mantelpiece . . . "I got back on dear Mamma and said Yes to Jim." She crossed and picked up the photo and handed it to Gemma.

"Meet my husband, Jim Willis, now out at the Rest, and probably as glad to be there as I am for him not to be here."

There was a pause, then again Janet said:

"As you see, we're a *very* nice family."

CHAPTER SEVEN

RATHER to her surprise Gemma found she fitted quite easily into Janet's household. She had expected the reverse, had seen herself holding back often from an unpleasant argument, giving in just for the sake of peace at all costs until she and Bruce lived their own lives, but it was not like that at all. Although Janet was sharp, candid frequently to embarrassment, touchy as a nettle, there was something about her that struck a chord in Gemma, made her respect and like the girl. She had a feeling that Janet unwillingly liked her in return.

"Do you find me a cross-current and a contradiction, Gemma?" Janet asked once.

"Yes," smiled Gemma cheerfully.

"You certainly don't mince words about it."

"Can one, to a cross-current and a contradiction?"

Harriet was now esconced in a corner of one of the stables.

"But don't go getting any bright ideas," warned Janet. "She can't grow up there."

"Why?"

"Well, for one thing she's not a milk type of cow calf. Did you know that?"

"Yes." Gemma remembered it from the Territorian.

"No, she's strictly the meat variety. Sorry to be brutal, but it's the truth. If she was intended for milk, she would grow large udders. She won't. She'll only grow large enough to feed her own calf."

"Well?" challenged Gemma.

"Well nothing. Everything at Mannering Park must account for itself. *You* will soon learn that."

"How do you mean?"

"Well, you won't be marrying Bruce just to sit there and be Mrs. Mannering junior, my dear Gemma, you'll have young Mannerings."

"I sincerely hope I do," said Gemma. "I love children."

"One child will do, so long as it's a male. If it's not" . . . Janet spread her hands, then said mischievously: "Offspring ad infinitum until you do."

"But I love little girls as well as little boys."

"It has to be a boy. Really, you are obtuse!"

"What," dared Gemma, "if a boy still never appears?"

"Deed poll," smiled Janet blandly. "My dear mamma did that. So long as the name of Mannering continues."

"You frighten me with Mamma."

"When you see her," said Janet cryptically, "you'll call me a liar."

On the second morning of Gemma's stay, Janet had asked Gemma could she ride.

"Pony club stuff only," Gemma had confessed.

"Better than nothing, I suppose. I'll get you a mount. Mother will expect me to do that at least. Incidentally, Mother still rides." Janet paused, then added: "Beautifully."

Janet was very critical of Gemma's horsemanship, but she was still glad that Gemma knew at least which

97

side of the mount to approach.

"I suppose you'll improve," she nodded. She asked abruptly: "How's your health?"

"Good. But what is all this? I'm not being put up for sale, am I?"

"Nothing would displease Mamma more than a fraile ladye. You look all right to me."

"Thank you," Gemma said wryly.

One night over dinner, Janet asked abruptly:

"Why did you accept Bruce?"

"I—I loved him."

"Loved Bruce?"

"He's very good-looking, very presentable, very elegant, very eligible."

"Thank you for the real reason at least," said Janet drily.

"Janet, that's unfair!" protested Gemma.

"It was more unfair of Bruce," scowled Janet. "You're quite a nice girl."

"How do you mean unfair of Bruce?"

"He was out on a limb at the time. I expect he felt the same as I felt when I married—" But Janet stopped herself from finishing that. "I suppose he felt he had to do something," she mumbled.

"Janet!"

"Sorry, I shouldn't have said that. It's a lie, any-way. Bruce fell for you. You can see that whenever he looks at you."

But lying was something that Janet could *not* do, and Gemma saw it at once. She accepted Janet's apology . . . an apology from Janet was so unknown you felt you had to accept it . . . but she remembered the exchange of words long after.

He was out on a limb. He had to do something.

Jim Willis came back from the Rest. Gemma had dreaded his return. If Willis's wife was touchy, then how would her husband be? But Jim Willis proved one of the nicest men Gemma had ever met.

His was a kind country face, a plain but endearing face, with soft brown eyes with a friendly glow in them. And he loved his Janet. For all that Janet had said ". . . as glad to be there as I am for him not to be here", Jim was still unmistakably and very obviously in love with his wife.

With the return of her husband, there was a change for the worse in Janet. She was more acid than ever; now there were no friendly breakthroughs with Gemma. Also she referred to Gemma to Jim as "she" or "her".

"She fetched a calf with her. Think out something for it, for heaven's sake." Or—"She can't ride for nuts. Give her some know-how."

Jim took Gemma out riding, and though in the beginning Gemma considered that Bruce should have polished her up in this, she soon knew she could not have had a better teacher. Jim was infinitely patient, infinitely encouraging, and he had a deep love for the country around him. Gemma was surprised to learn that he, too, was not country born.

"I'm not, but you can tell that. But you have that country look, Bill."

"No, I was a city sparrow. But I always had a feeling for the outdoors, so I came to perhaps the world's biggest outdoors of all. There are not many wider horizons than those of inland Australia "

"You came straight to Mannering Park?"

"Yes, and remained at Mannering Park. I worked myself through every single section of it, the stables, the machine shop, the book-keeping section, even the stock work. I did it all, from roustabout to station foreman."

"And then you married the boss's daughter."

"Yes. That finally set the seal." Jim's voice was both rueful yet proud at the same time, and Gemma knew the pride was because of Janet. "Ever tried a jump, Gemma?" he asked. "How about that very low log? Dandy will take you over."

At the other side of the log, after he had praised her, Jim said: "I married Janet because I loved her. Her being the boss's daughter was one of the unfortunate things that went with it, but when you love someone you take it all in your stride. I was a good worker, I knew that, and I knew that Mrs. Mannering couldn't pass that over when I asked her for Janet." A pause. "But I knew, too, that Janet didn't love me. She was all for the Torrance fellow. When you see him you'll know why."

"I've seen him," said Gemma.

"He was, of course, quite unthinkable for a Mannering, but Janet has told me that the tune is a little different now, that a change could be creeping in. Actually what she said" . . . a wry smile . . . "was 'I was born six years too soon'."

"Oh, Jim, she was joking." But Janet had said that, too, thought Gemma, to her.

Jim shrugged philosophically, then went on, "I didn't waste any time, Gemma, when I saw how Janet was reacting to the Torrance taboo, how the girl was ready for *anyone* who would pluck her from the Mannering tree. Janet was full of rebellion, and she only said Yes to me out of rebellion, but it still didn't worry me. I had no pride . . . is there pride in true love? . . . and I didn't mind being the afterthought. It didn't matter how I got Janet so long as I got her. I knew, too, that Janet's mother would agree . . . not enthusiastically, perhaps, but probably a little thankfully not knowing what her rebel daughter might do next.

"So we married." Jim smiled at Gemma, then said: "Shall we try that jump again?"

Bruce drove over every day to Janet's, and Gemma planned to surprise him, when she became more accomplished, by riding, not driving, over to him. But meanwhile she had a lot of faults to right, only small ones, but Bruce still might notice them, so the next day she drove her car across instead.

It was an excessively hot day, so Gemma hopefully put Harriet in the back seat. The drive might stir up a little wind, she thought, and the calf would certainly appreciate that.

Harriet looked overheated, uncomfortable and cross, and her pink mouth was open more often than shut as she tried to gulp in more air. Because of this she was dribbling, and Gemma looked disgustedly down on a wet splodge on her fresh green dress.

"Really, Harriet, you need a bib! Now I'll have to change."

She ran back to the house, and the run made her hotter still. On an impulse she took out her shorts and tube top.

When she got to Bruce's, Bruce was away at the

western fields. Gemma stopped for a while talking to Hannah, then decided to follow Bruce out there, give him a surprise. She would put Harriet out to graze when she got there; Harriet would enjoy that.

When she reached the western fields, she scouted around until she found a huddle of horses on the other side of the paddock. Near the horses were Bruce and his men, evidently, from the businesslike circle they had formed, conferring. She put Harriet out and let her delight in grass under her hooves instead of cement.

She had completely forgotten about her shorts and top. If she had remembered them, she would have congratulated herself on having the good sense to wear such suitable clothes on such a hot day.

She looked towards the horses and saw Bruce detach himself from the circle of stockmen. He was saying something to a young junior whom Hannah had told her earlier had only been signed on this week. Hannah had been interested in him, for he came from her old home town.

Presently Gemma saw that the boy was riding across to her. When he came up to her, he dismounted and touched his big hat. All the workers wore ten-gallon hats. The aboriginal stockmen particularly loved them.

"Mr. Mannering says it's too hot for you here, miss. He says to go back."

"Back?" she queried.

"Back to the homestead."

"But—" Gemma began.

"Also," said the boy, "to take the calf."

The young stockman was not looking at Gemma

now, he was doing something to his saddle. "That's what he told me to say, miss." He added a little uncomfortably: "I have to do what he says."

"Of course you do. Thank you. Will you help me push this child in the car? Then we'll go home."

"Thank you, miss."

The boy helped her, and Gemma reversed the car and drove back to Janet's again. She supposed she should be grateful for Bruce's consideration, but she would have preferred for him to have come and told her himself. Also, there had been a kind of hesitation in the boy, almost a reluctance to pass on the message. Or was it command? Still, it was very hot, and she supposed Bruce would know what these inland suns could do better than a new chum.

She put Harriet back in the corner that Janet had found for her, then went into the homestead, showered and changed into a cool shift.

And it was of the shift that Bruce spoke the moment he walked up the front steps and down the hall no more than twenty minutes later.

Janet and Jim were sitting in the lounge with Gemma by this, and Jim had mixed long cold drinks. Because it was such a hot day, Jim had put a cube of ice in each, and afterwards Gemma thought she would always remember what happened when Bruce walked in as something accompanied by the chink of ice, rather, she thought vaguely at the time, like incidental music to a movie.

"I must say, Gemma," Bruce burst out, "you do look better now in a dress. I know you're feeling our heat, but was it necessary to drive out there wearing an outfit like you did?"

Gemma was so startled that she spilled some of the drink down the dress that Bruce had just said she looked better in. She stared at Bruce.

"I've always worn shorts."

"In Sydney, yes. On the beach, yes. But this is not Sydney and it's not the beach."

"But it's a very hot day," she pointed out.

"You'll have to live with that, and live with it, I hope, in conventional clothes. Good lord, I trust I'm not a prig, but—"

"You are," Janet came in quite coolly and quite unemotionally . . . on the surface, anyway. "You've always been a prig. Of all the unnecessary fuss!"

"It's not unnecessary, and you know it. You know how Mother will react."

"I know how you're reacting." It was still Janet.

"Janet, keep out of this, it's nothing to do with you. You weren't there, I was."

"I should sincerely hope so, to be throwing such a filthy mood like this. I wouldn't like to think it sprang secondhand."

"I had ten of the stockmen around me, including the new boy. How do you think I felt when Gemma pulled up in—" Bruce gave a disgusted hunch of his shoulders.

"Pleased, I should think," said Janet, "that your wife has good legs."

"She's not that yet," he snapped.

"No." Gemma had found her tongue at last. "I'm not that yet."

That sobered Bruce a little. He turned and looked at Gemma.

"What you do in the house is different," he said

in a milder voice, "but no man wants—well—"

There was silence. No one in the room spoke. In the end it was Bruce who broke the quiet himself.

"It wasn't just what you were wearing, Gemma, it was the juvenile way you were behaving. I pride myself that I have a high status among the men. I make it a strict rule never to fraternize too much. And what do you do? You make a conversation piece of yourself. You follow me out, and when you find me you get out of the car and start skipping a calf. I tell you, I'll be the laughing stock of my own staff!"

"There was a bride who skipped a calf
To coax a laugh from the boss's staff."

Janet looked round delightedly, delighted at her own composition.

"Did you know I could write poetry, brother?" she giggled, taking no heed of Jim's restraining hand on her arm.

However, Bruce took no notice in his turn of his sister. His attention was on Gemma.

"We'll forget the shorts incident. You were not to know, I suppose. But, Gemma, you'll have to do something, or let us do something, about that beast."

"Harriet?"

"There you go again! You're determined to annoy me, aren't you?"

"No, Bruce, I'm not, and I'm sorry if you think that of me. But what can I do?"

"Seeing you won't agree to what's usually done, and should be done, then we'll take it bush and let it go."

"It couldn't survive. I haven't reared it to be self-sufficient. Besides, there may be dingoes."

"Well, you should have thought of that, shouldn't you?" Bruce went across to the corner bar and poured himself a drink.

There was another silence. This time it was Gemma who broke it.

"I'll take Harriet to Boothagullagulla," she said.

"What?" Bruce wheeled round.

"There's welcome on the mat there for Harriet." Now why had she said such a crazy thing? Bruce would only look contemptuous again.

But Bruce was too angry for contempt.

"Whom do you know at Boothagullagulla?" he demanded.

"Chris Mitchell."

"Since when?"

"Since the day I arrived here. I took the wrong turning."

"You certainly have a talent for doing the wrong thing, Gemma, meeting the wrong people. Whom else have you met?"

"I've met Tim Torrance." Gemma had risen. Her chin was out. "And if it's any consolation to you, *I* found him the wrong person, too."

She was aware that Janet was looking at her curiously, Bruce furiously, Jim with a friendly smile in his eyes.

But she was not waiting to find out what came after the curiosity, the fury, the friendship. There was something to be done at once. Harriet was to be taken at once, taken to Boothagullagulla where there was welcome on the mat.

Before any of them knew what she was doing,

Gemma had taken up the car keys, left the house, crossed to the barn, deposited Harriet once more in the back seat of her car, and started down the long track to the signpost with the two arrows.

She drove very fast, she did not want to be caught up by anybody, even by Jim, but by the fourth gate she saw that she was safe and that no one was following her.

She drove on to the arrows, then took the other direction, the track to the Mitchell homestead.

As she cleared its final gate, then closed it behind her, she saw that there was a lot of activity in the barns and stockpens beyond the friendly house with the wide rim of verandah. Coming closer, she saw that beasts were being loaded. She saw the large truck that would take the loads in relays to the road train waiting on The Bitumen, since a monster of the size of a road train could never negotiate a minor track.

She saw the sign on the truck: Territorian.

At the same time she saw Tim Torrance ... and he saw her.

He was in his old clothes again, oil-stained denims, black sweatshirt. He reached up into the truck and found a rag to wipe the worst of the dust and grime from his hands. He finished off by slithering the hands down the sides of his pants. Then he strolled across to her.

"Good afternoon, Future Mrs. Mannering."

"Good afternoon, Territorian. Still not trusting your men to do their stint without supervision? Still checking the process for time and expected production yourself?"

"I see the Mannering yeast is working on you already, you've achieved quite a Mannering edge. So" . . . he had taken out the makings and was rolling a cigarette . . . "the Establishment has won." He licked the edges of the paper together.

"I wouldn't be so free with words if I were you, you could be Mannering-snared yourself." What was there in this man that made her have to answer him back with better, or so she desperately tried, than he gave to her? Gemma thought. "Are you aware," she dared, "that as a person of means, many means, you are now not quite so unacceptable there as you were before?"

"Goody-goody!" He deliberately laid down the cigarette and clapped his hands. Big hands. Leather brown. Hard white knuckle bones.

His cool control of the situation on top of one of the worst afternoons she had ever had infuriated Gemma. She heard herself saying things she would not have dreamed of saying before.

"Where you were not quite the Establishment's dream for Janet, who knows, you could be for Vida . . . Stop, please, you're hurting me!"

"I could half kill you, you little fool, the flaming rot you say! Look at me, *look at me*, Future Mrs. Mannering, do you think anyone would stop me from taking what I wanted *if I really wanted it*? Do you?"

"I don't know."

"Then know this: I was not interested in Janet Mannering, nor she, if she would only think about it, in me. It was a simple case of elementary rebellion in her instance. Her marrying Jim Willis was another rebellious act, but one, happily, that will pay off."

"Then it hasn't."

"But it will," he said confidently. "I like Jim."

There was a mutinous pause, the mutiny from Gemma.

"You think you know everything, don't you?" she gritted.

"I know a great deal more than you," he retorted.

"Next you'll be telling me that Bruce also only suffered a rebellion when he—that is—"

He did not let her finish. "Yes," he said brutally, "he did."

"What?"

"You heard me. It was a temporary reaction, nothing else. Bruce Mannering doesn't love you, didn't love you, will not love you. Now how's that for knowledge?" He had taken up the cigarette again and his eyes behind the blue weave of smoke mocked at Gemma.

"I have nothing to say to you." She turned.

"You've already said it," he grinned hatefully.

"I brought Harriet to Chris." She felt she could not bear to follow up the other conversation.

"Sick of her?"

"No, but she'll be better here." Gemma started walking to the house.

In a moment he was walking beside her, a huge man with the easy lope of the horseman, even though his transport now was mostly thirty-six wheels.

"Chris isn't here," he said. "Isabel has dragged him down to Melbourne for some reason or other. But you can still leave the child. I'll fix up a place and tell Ludy."

"Thank you. I know Chris won't mind. He said

there'd be a welcome on the mat." Gemma paused, and her lip trembled. "For me as well." Now why had she added that?

At once she felt his hand, that big brown leather and white-knuckled hand resting on hers. It could have been to help her over a rough patch of the dirt path, but she knew it wasn't.

"That bad?" he asked quietly.

"Yes . . . no . . . oh, please—"

"Cry if you want to. No one will see. I can stand in front of you. That's one of the advantages of being a mountain."

"I'm not going to cry," she insisted.

"Good for you! Smile, then."

To her surprise she found herself actually managing a watery grin.

Tim Torrance grinned back.

"Now there's something to wipe that grin off," he warned. "If you think you're rid of me, along with Harriet, you best have another thought. What do you think of this?" He had reached in his stained work pants pocket and removed an envelope.

"Open it," he said.

Gemma did.

"Read it," he said.

Gemma did.

" 'The presence is requested'," she murmured aloud, " 'at the engagement party of Miss Gemma Glasson of Sydney and Mr. Bruce Mannering of Mannering Park of—' "

"Finish it."

"Of Mr. Timothy Torrance." Gemma looked up.

She had known about it, she had just hinted something of the sort to him about it, but she still hadn't really believed it. Not this man and the Mannerings.

"You wouldn't go," she said.

"Just wouldn't I!"

"You mean you're going?"

"Why not?" He had taken his hand away from hers again and once more he was eyeing her narrowly behind blue weaves of smoke. "You might remember," he taunted, "that I clean up well."

"Is it—Vida?"

"I'll tell you that when I look her over," he drawled.

"You're abominable!" she snapped.

"You get abominable answers when you ask abominable things. No, it's not Vida."

"Then the Mannerings." Janet had said that, had taken it as a matter of course that everyone would feel gratified at the thought of being connected with a Mannering.

"In a manner," he said shrewdly, "it would be the Mannerings."

There was a pause.

"I'll go now." Gemma turned.

"Yes. See you" ... he looked at the invitation ... "next Wednesday."

"It can't be then," she said. "Mrs. Mannering isn't back."

"She flew in an hour ago. I heard a Cherokee landing on the strip. Either the Flying Doctor or one of her neighbours ... certainly not Chris ... gave her a lift."

"She's back? Then I'd better leave at once."

"Yes, you'd better." He gave a taunting smile. "Goodbye, Future Mrs. Mannering. My regards to your mother-in-law. Tell her I haven't answered the invitation yet but that the reply is Yes."

"Do that yourself!" snapped Gemma crossly.

"In my uneducated fashion? In my clumsy hand? A thumbnail dipped in tar?"

She did not answer him. Nor did she go back to press a last kiss on Harriet, something she wanted to do very much.

She drove down to the arrows again, turned again, began the ritual of the gates. Then she drove past Bruce's towards Janet's, except that to reach Janet's you had to pass the big house, and this afternoon that was not to be.

Bruce was out signalling to her. Several cars were around. There was an air of activity, an air of importance. Doors were open, windows flung wide. It only needed, thought Gemma a little hysterically, for a flag to be flown, a house flag proclaiming: They're here. They're in residence.

She stopped the car.

Bruce ran across to her. "Darling, you had me worried. Mother and Vida are home—the F.D. dropped them at the strip. Mother can't wait to meet you. Please come at once. You look very nice in that dress, Gemma. But then you always do look nice." He was peering anxiously, eagerly, even wistfully at her.

. . . Do I? Gemma could have asked. Do I, Bruce, in shorts? But she didn't.

She got out, straightened her dress, then followed Bruce up the steps, longer steps, a larger verandah, a grander hall. Everything a little more elegant, a little superior.

"Mother is waiting for you in the lounge. In here, Gemma." Bruce pushed Gemma gently.

Gemma went in.

CHAPTER EIGHT

HOW had Gemma pictured Mrs. Mannering?

She could not have said.

Even though Janet had responded when Gemma had complained that she was being frightened by "Mamma" with a cryptic: "When you see her you'll call me a liar," Gemma still had conjured up nothing.

A nebulous figure, always very regal, always very grand, had risen before her, but still nebulous. No face at all.

Now Gemma faced Mrs. Mannering. And Mrs. Mannering was exquisite. Chiselled features. Perfectly groomed, faintly blued hair. Lovely *smiling* grey eyes, and if, in the words of some novelists, there was something else behind the friendly serenity of those smiling eyes, Gemma did not see it. A well preserved figure. An innate graciousness. "A real lady", Gemma could imagine people saying, for that was what Mrs. Mannering looked. A real lady.

"My dear," said Bruce's mother, and her voice was beautifully controlled. She did not rise, but she extended a cool pink cheek to Gemma, and Gemma went and kissed it.

Janet and Jim were already in the room. Bruce had come behind Gemma. A girl ... she would be Vida ... was estimating Gemma.

"Nice," she awarded at last. "The way Bruce was going on we didn't know what he would bring home."

"Vida!" Mrs. Mannering said it once only, but Vida was subdued.

"My ill-mannered younger daughter means you're a very pretty girl, Gemma," Mrs. Mannering excused charmingly. "Now come and sit beside me, dear. I'm sure we have a lot to say to each other."

Gemma went.

Then it all began.

It was unbelievable, Gemma thought dazedly afterwards, how Mrs. Mannering could praise yet at the same time damn. Damn faintly, indeed so faintly it could be your own imagination, and yet . . .

"How gloriously slim you are! Yet are you fit with it? Often it's otherwise, unhappily, and inland life is only for the robust. You're beautifully fair, aren't you, dear? A pity, perhaps. The sun does such damage to blondes, especially tawny ones. Tawny ones seem to invite the ray, I always think. Then up here we have to watch for skin cancers. Such a bore!

"Now about your godfather, dear, Mr. Bernard Drews—he was quite a figure, wasn't he, a really remarkable man. But not any consolation to you now, I expect, I mean not in worldly comfort, for they tell me that scientists are sadly unrewarded. And worldly comfort does count. Believe me, Gemma dear, since beef went down we pastoralists have learned that."

Gemma's parents came next. What profession had her father followed? How nice . . . though no doubt Gemma's mother must have sighed often for a more lucrative calling.

Gemma's school? Close attention to this.

Gemma's work? Well, all the girls these days were having careers, and she was glad, anyway, that

Gemma had chosen commerce, not modelling or acting, as many seemed to be doing of late, for where would modelling and acting fit in up here? But now that there had been a necessary reduction of staff she was sure that their book-keeper would be pleased with a little help at times.

Finally . . . and a little-girl smile that somehow did not look ridiculous on this mature woman . . . a more pleasant topic, Gemma my dear.

Dresses. What had Gemma brought for her engagement and wedding gowns?

That topic, thought Gemma dismally, might be pleasant to Mrs. Mannering, but it was not, in the circumstances, particularly pleasant to her.

She cleared her throat and began the sad saga of Harriet and the wedding outfit.

She did not mention Tim Torrance's part in the unfortunate episode, only the calf's.

"The driver handed me this calf," she said. She added hurriedly: "But Harriet—I mean the calf is gone now. I took it over to Mr. Mitchell's."

Up till then, Mrs. Mannering had received everything quite well, even inserted an amused little laugh here and there. But at the mention of Chris, she said sweetly but definitely to Gemma:

"We have very little to do with the Mitchells, dear. No, there's nothing you can put a finger on, save the inevitable boundary fence disagreement here and there, but they're such—well, dull people. Not—well, not our class of people at all. Just no standing, Gemma. Then that absurd Isabel with her ridiculous good deeds! Really, it's too ludicrous. I'm sorry you left the wretched thing there, but never mind, it's done now.

Tell me about your ill-fated dress."

"I made it myself." Gemma had been very proud of that fact, but she saw at once that Mrs. Mannering was patently unimpressed.

"Very sentimental, I'm sure, but for an occasion like a wedding I believe one needs a little more than love in every stitch." Mrs. Mannering touched Gemma's hand gently to show that there was no ill-will meant.

"What material, dear?" she begged prettily.

"A sort of lacy sheer."

"Oh, no!"

"Gathered and very full," Gemma went on.

"My dear Gemma, do you know what, I think your absurd calf did us a good deed after all. You must have something very straight, very regal, even severe, and, of course, embossed. A beautiful sculptured material that depends entirely on line. We'll send to David Jones at once."

"But—" Gemma began.

"Vida will check your size, and I'll write tonight. Now about your engagement party dress."

"That is intact," Gemma assured her.

"What is it, dear?"

Gemma told her, and this time received approval.

"Unsophistication by all means for an engagement. And I'm so relieved it's white, because I'm planning an entirely white function."

"What, Mrs. Mannering?"

"My mother," came in Bruce at this juncture, "does these sort of things beautifully. You'll be amazed, Gemma."

"Everything will be white," repeated Mrs. Mannering. "We'll write for white flowers, since we could never hope to supply those ourselves, not out here."

"If it was blue we could," Gemma said mechanically. She could not believe what was happening. "We could have Salvation Jane."

"That's a weed. No, gardenias, I think, orchids, roses. And you and the girls can get to work making mock waterlilies."

"Mock waterlilies?"

"Much as I would prefer the real thing, I doubt if a real waterlily could support a candle. You see, I intend to float these waterlilies, each with a lit candle in its cup, around our pool—that's where the party will be staged. Oh, Bruce dear, I will also want the little punt painted white. I plan to pile it high with white roses. Also I want—"

Gemma sat stupefied . . . stupefied was the only word she could have given to the way she felt.

"Guests will fly in from every state," continued Mrs. Mannering, "and of course we always fly in the caterers and the orchestra." A pause. "They, too, must wear white. White jackets or white tuxedos."

In a small disbelieving voice Gemma asked: "Who else besides the caterers and the orchestra will wear white?"

"*Everyone*. I told you, dear, it will be a white party. So virginal. So young and sweet. When I think how Bruce wanted—" A little shrug and a reproachful look at her son . . . but followed at once with an obviously disquieting thought.

"*You* haven't been married before, Gemma?"

"No." Gemma added dully: "Nor even engaged."

"So suitable. Now where was I up to?"

"White." It was Gemma again. Bruce was just standing there. Vida was still estimating. Jim Willis had slipped out. Janet's eyes were down.

"Oh, yes. All the ladies in white gowns as directed on the invitations," said Mrs. Mannering. "All the gentlemen in white suits as also directed."

"The men in white suits?" Gemma was now sitting very still. Again she was reading an invitation that a man in oil-stained pants and greasy sweatshirt had taken out of his pocket and handed to her.

The presence is requested ... Gemma Glasson of Sydney ... Bruce Mannering of Mannering Park ... of Mr. Timothy Torrance.

But she could not remember reading anything about dress.

"I don't think Gemma believes you." It was Janet, eyes up again, speaking drily, wryly, something enigmatical in her rather husky voice. "Haven't you seen the invitations, Gemma?"

"No. Yes. I mean—"

"Poor child, we're rushing her." It was Mrs. Mannering now, sweetly, tenderly concerned. "Show your dear girl the invitations, Bruce, and really, Bruce, I thought you would have done this before."

"I've been very busy, Mother." Bruce produced the same embossed card that the Territorian had, and passed it over. He looked sulky.

Gemma read it quickly. She already knew what it said. But what she wanted to know now was what she had *missed* ... if she had missed it.

Yes, she had. It was there quite clearly. Just after the date for the R.S.V.P. A chaste but unmistakable :
ALL WHITE, PLEASE, DEAR LADIES AND

GENTLEMEN. THANK YOU, ROBERTA MANNERING.

All Gemma could think for the moment was: "So her name is Roberta." Then she thought:

"*Him* in white! The savage in a white suit! He may clean up well, but I hardly think he'll clean up as well as that, as a thirty-six-wheeler in a white coat and white slacks! Not a man who answers his invitation with a thumbnail dipped in tar!" She felt very near hysterical laughter.

But she contained herself. She handed Bruce back the tasteful white invitation.

"It's very nice, Mrs. Mannering," she praised.

Back in the Willis house, where it had been decided she would stay until after the big day, Gemma made blindly for her bedroom, but she was stopped before she could get there by a convulsed Janet.

"If only you could have seen your face!" Janet started laughing again.

"Janet, Mrs. Mannering—your mother—she couldn't."

"My mother can, will, and it will be quite wonderful. You'll see."

"It sounds like a stage show," sighed Gemma ruefully.

"It will be pure opera. Classic opera. Everything will be in perfect taste. It will go off without a hitch. That's Mamma."

"Well, I must admit she is a remarkable woman."

"I told you so."

There was a small silence. Then Gemma said hopefully: "Also she seemed to like me."

"Look, Gemma, she loved you. Anyone previously

unmarried or unattached is manna from heaven to Mamma at this particular moment. I'm not saying a little money as well wouldn't have improved things, but—"

"But being unmarried is the first requisite?"

"Yes."

"Janet, I feel it only fair that I should know more. Was Bruce—was your brother—was he—"

"Yes," nodded Janet, not very concerned. "He was, or tried to be, entangled. I may as well tell you. Up here everyone tells everything in time, and you'll be sure to learn sooner or later."

"Learn what?" asked Gemma.

"That Bruce was badly smitten with a married woman. It's the first time I've ever seen him rebel against Mamma. I think he would even have gone ahead with it, too, only Jenny Lawson simply didn't care two hoots about Bruce."

"Jenny was the married woman?"

"Yes. She turned Bruce down."

"So—so he came to Sydney and asked me."

"Well, you could say that in a way, I suppose, if you weren't such an attractive girl," Janet said frankly. "No, I think Bruce was really taken with you, but I think, too, bringing someone home to spite Mother hurried it up quite a deal. But it didn't spite Mother after all. As you could see just now, it delighted her, even though you brought no welcome dowry. Mother is absolutely thrilled at putting all our talkative friends in their places by staging this white horror."

"You said it would be done beautifully."

"It will be. Everything always is. Take no notice of me."

"What happened to this Jenny?" Gemma asked after a pause.

"She eventually got rid of her husband. He was a pig, and I don't blame her."

"Through evidence with Bruce?" Well, thought Gemma, I have to know some time.

"Oh, heavens, no! Through the Territorian."

"Tim—Tim Torrance?"

"Yes. He's no good, you know," Janet said quite cheerfully. "After encouraging Jenny to go ahead, he faded out quick-smart when she followed his advice and did. There was quite a scandal about it—poor little girl left high and dry and all that. That's when Bruce stepped in with his offer, and poor Mother had kittens. But Jenny wouldn't look at Bruce. She finally married another man, and, or so they say, is living happily ever after."

"I just can't believe it," said Gemma.

"Don't tell me you thought the wicked world stopped at Sydney!" Janet laughed again, then resumed.

"Our dear Mamma was thankful when it was all over, and that, I think, is why she has greeted you with such very wide open arms. Such relief, Gemma, to have someone sweet, unsullied and unmarried. But the thing that really bugs me is her change of attitude over the Territorian. He was taboo for me, and should be, on the basis of his history with Jenny Lawson, for Vida. I mean what's expected of you for Bruce should be expected of Tim for V. But it's entirely different now for Vida. The reason, of course, is the fall in beef and the Territorian's millions." Janet's laugh was now brief and dry and unamused. "Did you know," she said, "that Mother has actually invited him to your 'do'?"

"Oh," replied Gemma. She found she could not say Yes, she found she could not say No, so she just left it at that. At: "Oh."

"Yes, she has invited the Territorian to Mannering Park. History is being made. And you just stand and say 'Oh'."

"I'm sorry, Janet."

"There'll be members of parliament here, heads of state, a baronet or two."

...And a man in oil-stained pants and a sweat-shirt, Gemma thought.

"There'll be dress rehearsals," Janet went on, "Bruce will carry a stopwatch to check the timing of everything. Jim will supervise a party of carpenters for the bachelor and spinster digs in the barns. The engagement cake will be flown in ... no, my dear, no home-made touch for an occasion like this.

"And you and Vida and I will make countless waterlilies. We'll put holes in them to support a candle. At the rehearsed moment all lights will be put off and only the candlelight remain."

"Janet, please stop!" begged Gemma.

"But it will be very romantic, Gemma," baited Janet relentlessly, "perhaps more romantic still if you'd brought some money with you, dear. But not to worry, when the Territorian meets our Vida's eyes across a candlelit pool, across a punt piled with roses, we won't be worrying about Bruce's bride and what she *didn't* bring, not with the road boss's millions."

"Janet!" Gemma said it quite sharply now.

"Yes, Janet, you've gone a bit too far." It was

123

Jim. Neither of them had seen him join them.

"It's the truth, though, isn't it?" Janet was a little hysterical by now. "Everyone in the Establishment has to bring something. Gemma brought her innocence. Even you, Jim, brought something. You came along with know-how, faithful service, the promise of faithful service in years to come."

"And I brought love," Jim said solidly, his eyes never wavering from his wife's.

With a strangled little cry, Janet ran outside.

Jim did not speak for a while. He crossed to the bar and mixed two drinks, then handed one to Gemma.

"I think you need this. I know I do."

Gemma felt she did need it, and she drank it gratefully.

"You don't want to take it too seriously," Jim advised presently.

"Didn't you when it was you?"

"I was spared a lot. After all, a Mannering daughter was not a Mannering son, and after all, a foreman, or manager, you name it and I'll answer to it, was not exactly a first prize."

"*I* think you were a first prize, Jim," Gemma said sincerely.

"Thank you, Gemma, and I think that Bruce is getting the very top of the class."

"After those mutual compliments," smiled Gemma, "tell me how you kept a straight face dressed all in white."

"I told you, we didn't have all that. But I also just told you not to take it that seriously."

"I have to. We all have to. You, too, have to wear

white."

"I quite like white," Jim said amicably. "It's a perfect choice for these latitudes. Oh, come, Gemma, don't make such a fuss."

"I was just wondering if—everyone likes white."

"When commanded, yes."

"But ones who are used to commanding themselves?"

"Namely?"

"Oh, no one in particular," evaded Gemma.

"Then we'll have to see, won't we?" smiled Jim. "Now I'm going out to see to my wife. Cheer up, girl, it's going to be fun."

"Yes," said Gemma, "it's going to be fun."

But when he had gone she went to the window and thought: Whose fun? When do I start to laugh?

She laughed the next day, though, over the waterlilies. One thing Gemma had never been able to make was knicknacks. Her waterlilies might be plastic, but they certainly wilted as though they were the real thing.

"Do something else, Gemma," Mrs. Mannering commanded impatiently at last.

All the guests to the party would be accommodated overnight at Mannering Park. There were the four houses available, and after that the barns, under Jim's supervision, were being partitioned to provide the single accommodation.

"Single girls, too?" Vida asked. "I've invited several."

"Only after the houses are exhausted, I don't like the idea of girls out there."

"They will," Vida grinned, but wiped away the

smile smartly.

"We will try the houses first," Mrs. Mannering said stiffly. "Of course the girls will have to double up, they will have to room together."

"Then Deborah can share with me," Vida decided.

"Deborah?"

"I went to school with her, remember?"

"Yes, I remember. Her grandparents were the Adelaide Stockleys."

"Yep. Filthy rich."

"I wish you wouldn't speak so disgustingly, Vida."

"And now," continued Vida, "Deborah is sole heiress. Her doting grandparents missed a generation and chose Deb. Deb is simply rolling."

"Vida! But yes, I suppose you can have her with you." Mrs. Mannering was looking rather thoughtful.

"What if she casts her eyes in the same direction as I'll be casting?" Vida said slyly.

"You're an impossible girl! Sometimes I think all my children are impossible. Now get on with those waterlilies. And Gemma, you can help me plan the menu. It has to be posted down tonight."

Gemma went obediently into Mrs. Mannering's exquisite writing room and sat down at a very beautiful desk. She was completely awed at the selection of viands that Mrs. Mannering wrote down and directed to be flown up.

"What did you expect, dear," Mrs. Mannering asked, looking up and catching a bemused look on Gemma's face, "a dormitory tea?" She laid her pen down for a moment. "You are a very naïve girl," she sighed, "absolutely no sophistication. Knowing you were from Sydney I had expected better."

"Better?" queried Gemma.

"I really meant more poise, dear. More maturity. I really don't believe you're as old as Vida."

"Oh, I am, I'm—"

"I know." Mrs. Mannering was characteristically impatient, she would never accept correction. "Now after the paté I think—"

On and on it went, and every day was the same. At times Gemma thought: If an engagement is like this, how will I get through a wedding? She longed often to escape, to jump in her little car . . . she was not efficient enough yet to leap on the back of a horse . . . and to seek out Chris. She thought often of Chris Mitchell and the comfort he had given her. She thought of the Territorian, too, but never in terms of comfort.

Meanwhile the big day came closer and closer. There were dress rehearsals, with Bruce timing everything to the second. Timing the moment the candles would be lit. Timing the moment the band would strike up. Timing the moment the fireworks would begin. Timing the moment Bruce and Gemma would toast each other, then all the rest of the guests, the diplomats, the heads of state, the what-have-yous, raise their glasses as well.

Sometimes Gemma thought she would explode. It was all so unreal, so pointless, so artificial, even though Bruce and Janet assured her that it would turn out, as everything their mother did always turned out, a triumph. Of all things at these times, Gemma longed for soft peaked ears lined with pink plush, an india-rubber nose, clumsy feet. She longed for Harriet. How big, she wondered, was Harriet now?

But there was no hope of escape. Every day brought more things to be done, more timing, more rehearsals, more fittings. Then on the day before the party the hairdressers were flown in.

That looked after that day, and, waking up the next morning, Gemma found that it was a beautiful morning. Somehow she had expected it *not* to be. You can't have everything go right, she had thought.

"Mother can." Gemma must have spoken aloud, for Janet, who had entered silently with an early cup of tea for Gemma, smiled crookedly. "It's usually amiable weather this time of the year, and besides, Mamma has been in close touch with the appropriate bureau. You could say in a way that she's even *ordered* a fine day."

At noon the planes began putting down on the Mannering Park strip. Gemma knew that people came to picnic races like this, but she had never dreamed that they came, too, to private parties. Yet one after the other, Bruce and Jim signalling them in by mirrors, by strips laid down between upturned white plastic buckets, by a fire lit to show the wind direction, Cherokees, Cessnas and Beachcraft, other small size planes, began to arrive. If Gemma had not been so amazed, she could have been nervous. All these important people! But she was too incredulous for nervousness.

Dusk was at seven. Up here in the sub-tropics, night fell instantly, no purple warnings, no gathering of pansy clouds. One moment bright blue skies, the next navy blue. But with the darkness now came light, the light of a hundred lanterns placed cunningly round the garden and round the swimming pool. At the right moment the lanterns would be extinguished and the candles on the floating waterlilies would light the scene instead. The punt with its load of white roses would drift gently over the sparkling water.

But just now it was party arrival time. The married guests, after being housed in the bungalows, their daughters after being doubled in any other available rooms, their sons after being shown the improvised cubicles in the barns, were strolling from their sleeping places for tonight to merge and mingle on the perfect Mannering lawns . . . and yes, *yes*, Janet was right. Bruce was right. What had sounded preposterous actually looked wonderful. Men and women moving around all in white. A white night. A white world.

Mrs. Mannering stood on a small flowered dais in a gown that had to be French. Vida stood beside her. Gemma had been told to wait in the wings, as it were.

"Your turn comes afterwards, my dear."

The white-jacketed orchestra was playing. White-jacketed waiters were moving quietly through the throngs.

It was all very wonderful, very exciting, and Gemma actually caught her breath over it.

Then she was letting her breath go, releasing it in horror and disbelief. How could he? *How could he?* How could the Territorian do this?

For Tim Torrance had just entered, and in that glittering white array he stood out like a beacon. Or the Devil? For though formally dressed, he was *darkly* dressed. He wore a black dinner suit.

Gemma was near enough to Mrs. Mannering to hear her angry: "The impertinence! Who does he think he is!"

Then she heard Vida whimpering: "But, Mother, you did agree . . . and Mother, remember—"

Tim Torrance was coming straight across to his hostess. His manners, anyway, left nothing to be desired. Also the manner in which he kissed Mrs. Mannering's hand would have passed anywhere. Except, and Gemma tried to step further back in the shadows, as he did so he looked straight at her as she stood in the "wings". And winked.

Then he straightened again.

"Mr. Torrance, I did request if possible—" Mrs. Mannering evidently found she could not stop herself at least from saying that.

"White gear? Sorry, but my only white stuff is a pair of overalls, and I hardly think— But" . . . an impudent grin . . . "I knew it was me you wanted, not the clobber, so here I am." He had turned slightly and now his glance fell on Vida.

"Hi there, kid," he dismissed.

For that was what it was, a dismissal, a dismissal of all Mrs. Mannering's plans. It was the final telling blow. Mrs. Mannering might forgive a black suit, a frivolous explanation as to why no white one had been forthcoming, especially when the explanation came from a man of such means, but his breezy "Hi, kid" to Vida made it quite clear, quite definite, to Vida's mother that as far as Tim Torrance was concerned what he represented in the way of success and wealth would never be of any concern of Mannering Park.

Mrs. Mannering's cool grey eyes were flaming un-coolly. Tim Torrance's own eyes accepted her chill with sly amusement.

"Having turned up," he drawled, "I'll now duly depart. Best of luck to the reason for all this." He looked around him briefly. "Goodnight to you."

As quickly and as suddenly as he had come, Tim Torrance was gone.

Mrs. Mannering was petrified for one second only. Then she turned sharply to Vida. "Pull yourself together, for heaven's sake! Mingle. Find Deborah. Really, Vida, you are a fool of a girl!"

Gemma slunk away. At any moment she would be called upon by Mrs. Mannering, or Bruce, or someone, to do something, say something, and just now—

It was at that moment she saw that there was worse still to come. She saw the girl, recognized the girl, then froze to the ground. She must be Vida's school friend Deborah, the girl Vida had chosen to room with her, the girl Mrs. Mannering had been interested in when she remembered her rich grandparents.

But she was also—someone else. She was that tall, very elegant, very attractive young woman that night in the Alice Springs hotel lobby, the girl who had stood near Tim.

There was no mistaking Deborah—*Deborah*, not Bush Betty, not Clara, not Tessie. Deborah Stockley might be an heiress, but she still had an eye for opals ... *or men*? In the end, to escape her, the Territorian had said to Gemma:

"Darling, you've been hours, but it's been worth every second." He had studied her proudly ... *mock* proudly ... up and down.

Afterwards in the dining room he had grinned back when Gemma had objected, and retorted:

"Mistress, fiancée, wife. That was the idea. Any of

the three would do so long as she got the message that you belonged."

And now the girl was here. Deborah Stockley was here at Gemma's engagement party to Bruce Mannering. Deborah had seen Gemma with the Territorian. She had watched him kiss her . . . put a ring on her finger.

At that moment Deborah turned, stared, loosened her arm from Vida's, then came across.

"Why, it's Mrs. Torrance," she smiled. "I met you at The Alice."

She extended a slender hand.

CHAPTER NINE

"YOU'RE mistaken. I'm not Mrs. Torrance," Gemma said coolly, and wondered how she could be so composed.

"Then engaged to be. Or—" A guilty clap to her mouth and a small girl look. "I *am* awful," Deborah Stockley apologized.

Vida had followed her friend across the lawn.

"Gemma, this is Deborah Stockley. I spoke about Deb, remember? Deb, this is Bruce's fiancée, Gemma Glasson. The reason for tonight's festivities." Vida tried to sound gay, but she still looked stunned.

"Of course. What a fool I am! I thought I'd seen Miss Glasson before. I thought I'd seen her with Mr. Torrance at the Alice Springs Hotel. Now that I take a second look I can see it's only a resemblance. Will you please forgive me, dear?"

"Yes," Gemma murmured.

Vida, still smarting, asked vindictively: "But you *did* see Tim Torrance?"

"I certainly did. And in a decidedly compromising situation. And to think, Miss Glasson, I mistook *you* for— Well, you understand."

Vida was not listening, not noticing the exchange of looks between the two girls. "That would be Torrance," she said, "he always had a reputation. There was Jenny Lawson . . . probably many before Jenny. Like silk purses out of pigs' ears, it seems you

133

can't make a gentleman out of a thirty-six-wheeler. Gemma, Mother is looking around for you. I think there's going to be an announcement."

Gemma, still managing to appear composed, nodded and threaded her way to the flowered dais. Bruce was already waiting there, so this must be the point of no return. Oh, for heaven's sake, why had she thought that?

The rest of the evening was sheer torment for Gemma, but for Mrs. Mannering it was a triumph. As though to make up for the one sour note, everything went perfectly. The lanterns went out at the right time, not one of the waterlily candles misbehaved, the music burst through gladly, the food was perfect, the wine was potent, the fireworks exciting, and Bruce and Gemma linked arms in the European manner and looked very picturesque as they plighted their troth.

There were congratulations from right and left ... most of them for Mrs. Mannering.

"Roberta, you should have been an entrepreneur."

"Roberta, you've excelled yourself."

No one mentioned a dark evening suit. Probably if they had, it would have only been to congratulate Mrs. Mannering again for affording them a moment of contrast. Drama, they would have called it, Gemma decided vaguely, vague because she wasn't thinking much about it, either, she was thinking only of Deborah Stockley.

She knew it would only be a matter of time before Deborah spoke to her again, and her heart sank. What could she answer to the girl at the next interrogation? What was she to do?

Janet came in with hot milk before Gemma put

out her light that night . . . no, it was the next morning. She sat on Gemma's bed with a mug herself, and grinned at Gemma.

"It went well."

"Very well," Gemma agreed.

"I wasn't there when Diablo appeared," Janet went on.

"Diablo?" Gemma queried.

"Oh, Gemma—Tim, of course. But I saw him prior to his appearance outside. What a man! You know" . . . a little tentatively . . . "he did something to me tonight as well as to Mamma. He made me see myself as I am, not as I *thought* I wanted to be."

"What do you mean, Janet?"

"He called: 'Hullo, Janet, still looking for gold windows when you have them at home?' and suddenly —well, I understood. I said: 'No, Tim,' and he smiled, and I smiled. He's wonderful, but" . . . a shake of Janet's head . . . "not my kind of wonderful, Gemma. Gemma, you wretch, you're asleep!"

Gemma wasn't, but she kept up the pretence. She had enough on her own plate just now without any offerings from Janet.

The day after the engagement party was almost as hectic as the day itself had been. There were guests to see off, to thank again for the gifts that Gemma had still not examined . . . and dreaded examining. There were gay responses to be made to their: "See you soon, Gemma, so build up your strength, next time it's for keeps."

There were things left behind that had to be hurried out to a departing plane. Kisses. Handshakes. Smiles. More thanks.

The caterers flew out. The orchestra flew out. Jim put a small army of stockmen to clean up the strip, the lawns and the pool. Gemma saw a load of dead roses being carted to the incinerator, and it did something odd to her. At the moment she could not understand the feeling. Afterwards she knew that those dead roses were the end, too, of something else.

Everyone relaxed the following day, tired, a little edgy, somehow let down as you often are let down after something is over. Then life went on again.

Not quite the same, though. A few of the more intimate guests had stayed on. Mrs. Mannering had suggested to Vida that she ask Deborah to stop.

"Poor Vida," Roberta Mannering said to Gemma, "he certainly crushed her, so she'll need company."

"Mr. Torrance?"

"Yes. But no more of him, please, Gemma. I never want to hear his name again."

Gemma was pleased to find that Mrs. Mannering also was not yet in the mood to discuss the next big function, that of the wedding, for she knew she was unready for it herself.

"I think," said Bruce's mother sweetly, "we'll all catch our breath first, take a well-earned rest."

The relief to Gemma was so great, it never occurred to her to wonder why Bruce made no protest. Down in Sydney he had been anything but a laggard lover. Now he was as apathetic . . . no, resigned was a nicer word . . . as she was.

Bruce was busy directing the northern section of the stock rounding-up these days; after the beasts were brought in to Mannering Park, Bagsworth . . . or Maloney . . . would take over and road train them south.

Deborah, when she was told of this aspect of outback life, insisted upon going,, too, to watch. She pleaded with Bruce to take the three girls, Vida, Gemma, herself.

Janet, who had been present when Deborah made her plans, said afterwards to Gemma:

"Watch yourself. There's a catch."

Of course there was a catch. Gemma was acutely aware of that. She knew that Deborah was only waiting for an opportunity to have a talk with her. It seemed incredible that the girl had not found an opportunity before, not in a remote cattle station like this, but Gemma had kept strictly to Janet's house, and the only time she had gone to the Mannerings', she had gone with others, and had never been alone with Vida's guest. However, out there in the northern section there should be plenty of chances, chances for Deborah to say—

"Yes," went on Janet darkly, "that girl is going to make a fool of you."

"What do you mean, Janet?"

"Look, Gemma, Jim might have gone to work on you, but you still can't ride for nuts. Not really. I've seen her ladyship ride. She's superb."

"Oh," Gemma said, relieved at Janet's reason for watchfulness.

"It's not that I mind one way or other," Janet continued with a shrug that meant it was obvious she did not mean, "but I hate seeing lambs taken to slaughter."

"Am I a lamb?"

"You're newly born compared to Deborah Stockley.

Oh, I know you're twenty-six to her twenty and a bit, but my, how that bit counts! I like you, Gemma. I think you could do better than my brother, but I still don't want you hurt."

"Thank you, Janet."

Again Janet shrugged.

The next day what Janet had said came true. Probably because she had been put on her mettle, Gemma rode worse than ever through sheer nervousness; she had never been quite so bad. Beside Vida, she made a pitiful show. But beside Deborah, she looked, as Janet had said she would look, a fool. She could see that Bruce was plainly dismayed.

Deborah was sweet about it, however, even though while she was being solicitous and helpful she still was putting Arab, her big black horse, through some very difficult . . . and showy . . . paces.

After lunch, when Gemma laboriously climbed up on Frenchy, when Vida hooked a leg over Paulette and hauled herself on, Deborah simply vaulted herself up to Arab. She was absolutely fluid, a really magnificent poppy of a girl, and Bruce's eyes followed her everywhere.

During the afternoon, things came to a head. Not the talking things that Gemma had dreaded, but the active things. Like riding.

There was a stampede. Bruce called it a "rush".

The three girls and Bruce were at the side watching the mob's progress under Bert, the head stockman. There was a thick pall of dust, but everything seemed to be going quietly.

Then something happened. A stir somewhere, a blown leaf, someone speaking in too loud a voice. Then it was on. The mob was churning around, dust was whirling, stockmen were racing in to bring back order, the dogs were doing their bit.

But Frenchy, insufficiently disciplined by Gemma, was galloping away from it all, galloping crazily, and Gemma knew she would never stay on.

It was just as she braced herself to fall that a hand took her rein and halted Frenchy. Gemma thought stupidly that it would be just the sort of thing for a film, instead of the desert hero, Bruce . . . except that in this instance it was Deborah saving her.

They all went home after that, and at Janet's villa Bruce said what Gemma had known he would.

"My dear Gemma, I know you want to please me, but I don't think you're up to this class of riding."

"No, Bruce, I'll stay at home tomorrow."

"Good girl, it will really be a relief to know you're back here and safe."

Janet had strolled in.

"What happened?" she asked.

"There was a bit of a rush, and Frenchy took off."

"What caused the rush?"

"Oh, good heavens, Janet, anything causes a rush with touchy cattle. You know that."

"Like a stirrup rattle?"

"Or a loud voice or a blown leaf or anything of the sort," said Bruce irritably.

"Like a stirrup rattle," nodded Janet. After Bruce had gone, she added: "Deborah's stirrup."

"Oh, Janet!"

"It's true. She's putting the skids under you, Gemma."

"If your mother was here she'd say why did I send

Janet to an exclusive college?"

"Well, she won't say why did I send Vida, because the answer will be to land something like Deborah."

"She's beautiful," blurted Gemma.

"And a snake. Well, don't say you weren't warned."

"I won't say it . . . but, Janet, I still can't do anything. You—you see—"

"Yes?"

Gemma looked away wretchedly. "I—I can't tell you."

"You're already married?" pounced Janet hopefully.

"No."

"Secretly engaged?"

"No."

"Then you love someone else?"

That was not so easy to answer. Gemma turned abruptly, leaving Janet to reach her own conclusion, and went to her room.

When she got there she sat a long time at the window. Why didn't I reply to Janet just now? she asked herself. I don't love anyone else. I can't. Then she heard herself whispering something that Janet had said before the party. "He's no good, you know", Janet had told her. She had been speaking of the Territorian.

But why, Gemma wondered, was she remembering that now, and why did it matter whether he was good, bad or indifferent? He had nothing to do with her, or she with him, so that closed the matter.

Slowly, so slowly that it did not seem to be happening, an insidious change crept in.

The wedding was never mentioned now, neither by Mrs. Mannering nor Bruce.

Bruce was away with the mobs quite a lot, and Vida and Deborah always accompanied him. After the rush incident there was no need for any excuse for leaving Gemma at home. The first time Mrs. Mannering had said: "It would be wiser to wait until you're more skilled, dear," but following that she said nothing at all.

The engagement gifts had been packed away, where, Gemma neither knew nor cared. She did not care, either, that she had not seen them. As a matter of fact she cared about nothing lately . . . except Harriet, and, of course, Chris. But the Mitchells were still in Melbourne. Bruce had said so. He had had cause to ring up Boothagullagulla about some fencing detail and had been told they were still away.

Gemma's heart had sunk. While Chris was as near as next door, even though that was a distance away, she had felt comforted. Now she felt bleak.

During the second week following the party, Mrs. Mannering began saying little things . . . significant things . . .

"If ever I saw a girl born to be the mistress of a station, it's Deborah."

Then: "Deborah was telling me how her grandparents favoured her in their will instead of their own son. Of course Deborah will inherit from her parents, too, later on. She's an only child. Such a young girl already to have so much money, yet so much more to come."

Later: "What a strong, active type Deborah is. I always think dark hair indicates resilience in a woman, and she certainly is a raven-haired beauty."

Gemma always agreed. It meant nothing to her. She knew the ending now as surely as she knew day from night, and she knew, too, that as far as she was concerned there was no pain attached, only the embarrassment of waiting for it all to happen. She knew she could have made it happen at once, spared everyone the discomfort of that unnerving wait. She could have gone to Bruce and said: "We were too hasty." He would have agreed, agreed with relief, that was very obvious, but something still stopped Gemma. She could not have said what it was.

But Deborah could, and did. Deborah sought her out the following morning, and after all the watching it came as a vast relief.

"Gemma, I've been waiting for you to come to me, but it seems I have to come to you."

Gemma heard herself say coolly: "Which one of us is Mahomet and which one is the mountain?"

"We won't go into that, but we will go into the time I saw you in the Alice Springs hotel."

"But you didn't. Remember? It was ony a resemblance." Gemma wondered at her blandness.

"It was you." Deborah said bluntly. "No need for subterfuge now. You were with Tim Torrance."

"So were you."

"Oh, no, I *tried* to be, but he shook me off. I was piqued at the time. I'm considered exceedingly attractive. And then I saw you."

"Go on, Deborah."

"You're attractive, too."

"Thank you."

"To some people. Evidently to him."

"Him?" queried Gemma.

"The Territorian."

"Go on, Deborah," Gemma invited again.

"I intend to." A pause. "And shall I also tell you what I intend to do later?"

"If you want to."

"I intend to marry Bruce Mannering. He attracts me, and I certainly attract him." A little low laugh.

"But most attractive of all," continued Deborah, "I find the prospect of being the future Mrs. Mannering of Mannering Park. Which the junior Mrs. Mannering must be, in time."

"I expect so."

"It appeals to me tremendously. I find Roberta's role very absorbing. I like to be the leader, the decision-maker."

"Bruce—"

"Will never be. His mother has seen to that. He'll be glad to have me take over."

"You sound as though you've taken over already," commented Gemma drily.

"It's only waiting for you now, Gemma. You must make the next move."

"What?"

"Oh, come, you don't love Bruce. You never did. You don't even like this place. You want to get away, but you can't make the break." There was another pause. A sly one. "And I know why."

"Then if you do, it's more than I know," Gemma said miserably.

"But you're still aware of a reluctance to leave, aren't you?"

"I—I—Well, yes," Gemma admitted with difficulty.

Deborah smiled thinly. "If the Mitchells were here, I think you would leave regardless."

"Regardless?"

"Of that odd reluctance you somehow feel but still can't explain. You would go to Boothagullagulla so that you didn't have to desert the inland entirely, so that you didn't have to close the gates."

"Close the gates?" echoed Gemma.

"Go south," impatiently. "Leave the top end."

"You're right," Gemma said in wonder. How did this girl know when she had not known herself?

As though she had asked the question aloud, Deborah shrugged: "I've studied you. I think I know more about you than you know yourself."

"Why have you studied me?"

"To get rid of you, of course."

"You could have done that the next morning after the party. You could have gone to Bruce and his mother and said: 'Miss Glasson was at The Alice with Torrance. I don't know in which capacity!'"

"Yes, I could have done that, but I wanted it done differently. I'll be living here, and I want no word of criticism. Any break must come from you. I know these country places. I know how things can be misconstrued, blown up out of all proportion, and you, Miss Glasson, the loser as well as being fair and small and fragile-looking, would undoubtedly emerge the winner. The talk would be that Bruce turned you down for me, and some...*many*...wouldn't like that at all. So you have to do the fading out, Gemma. You'll be gone, so it won't matter if there are any fingers pointed at you. If there is any talk you won't be here. Well"...a sly smile..."not directly here."

Gemma looked at her bewildered. "But why should it be me? Bruce is in this, too."

"I just told you. It would suit all of us, you, Bruce, me, for the affair to dwindle out without any heroics."

"How would it suit me?"

"I told you that, too. You just don't want to leave up here. Not deep down, Gemma. No, I didn't take psychology or anything like that, I just know. If there's a showdown, you'll have to leave. If there's a gradual easing, you can bow gracefully out and go across to your friends the Mitchells, who, I've been told, are expected back at the end of the month."

"You have it all worked out," said Gemma drily.

"I've always worked things out. We'll keep on as we are now, and finish the affair in a nice civilized manner. Mrs. Mannering, I know, would be embarrassed with any other way, and even though she obviously wants me for Bruce, for my potential as a future mistress of Mannering Park as well as my money, she would still hate a scene. Bruce would, too. He's that type."

"The girls—"

"Vida is weak as water, and Janet—well, she married the foreman." Deborah yawned, smiled blandly and left Gemma staring dazedly after her.

But not for long.

I may be naïve, but there comes a time when there's an end to naïveté, Gemma said, dazed no longer, and she straightened her shoulders.

She packed her bags. She got out her car. She went across to Mrs. Mannering and bade her a polite good-bye . . . and had the satisfaction of seeing Mrs. Mannering for once not able to find any words. She left a message for Bruce, just a very brief one.

"Best wishes. Gemma."

She did not seek out Vida, and she had already finished with Deborah. She would have liked to have said goodbye to Jim. Janet she could not bear to think about. She took out a scarf that Janet once had admired, and running back to the house she placed it on Janet's dressing table. Thank heaven the girl was not there. Gemma turned and ran back again.

She stopped at Bruce's villa to see Hannah. Hannah was in tears because she had learned that she would probably not be needed in the future.

"Who said so, Hannah?"

"That was what upset me. She did."

"She?"

"That Miss Stockley staying at the big house. Where does she think she comes in?"

"I believe she does come in, Hannah, but not to worry, we'll think of something." Gemma kissed her, and left.

Although the Mitchells were still away, she intended calling in before she hit south. I must see Harriet, she thought foolishly, I must touch that india rubber nose just once again.

She went through the Mannering Park gate ritual, then she went through the Boothagullagulla gate ritual, only in reverse.

The homestead was shut up. Even Ludy did not appear to be there. Gemma left the car on the drive and hurried towards the barns.

"Harriet!" she called.

At once she heard movement, and someone put a head over the lower door of the first outbuilding.

"No Harriet here," called a voice. "She lives in the end villa. But would I do instead? Name of Tim."

The Territorian pulled the bolt of the door and stepped outside. He looked Gemma up and down and his glance was searching, probing.

"You forgot," he said at last, the glance reaching, then focusing on Gemma's left hand, "to return the ring."

CHAPTER TEN

GEMMA stood aghast. She *had* forgotten, she saw.

But how had this man known she had left Mannering Park for all time, had closed the chapter called Bruce?

"Up here a wind will blow even a change of mind," Tim Torrance grinned. "And yours is more than that, isn't it, it's a change of heart. Come in and tell me all about it." He pointed to the barn behind him, and Gemma saw that there were a couple of chairs, a table with some cups, a jug.

"The Mitchells—" she asked.

"Are still away. Chris would like me to use the homestead when I'm around these parts, but I prefer here. Tea?"

"Thank you." Gemma sat down. She was still stunned about the ring. How could she have not remembered that most important thing of all?

"What can I do about it?" she fretted.

"The ring?"

"Yes."

"Keep it," he advised.

"Oh, no!"

"Then I'll get one of the stockies to ride over with it for you. I'd go myself, only I doubt if I'd be welcome at the Establishment."

"Can you blame Mrs. Mannering?"

"Yes. Personally I've always liked penguins better

148

than doves. I believe most people prefer black and white to all white."

"I meant—"

"I know what you meant. But better to scotch something right from the beginning than to build up a maiden's hopes. Or" ... slyly ... "her mother's hopes. As regards the penguin, you must admit I stood out that night."

"Like the devil." Janet had called him Diablo.

"I was different," he grinned.

"You were abominable!"

"What else did you expect from a thirty-six-wheeler? You must admit it took courage."

"Your courage didn't last, evidently. You left at once."

"I had seen," he smiled, "a certain faintly recalled figure."

"So you deserted?"

"What good would I have done?"

"You could have supported me," said Gemma.

"When you were going to deny everything? Oh, yes, you were. Supporting a denial would have only emphasized the fact that Bush Betty was spreading the truth."

"You were very wrong with her, too. She's extremely rich, comes from a good family and her name is Deborah Stockley."

He whistled. "So she's a Stockley."

"*Now* she is."

"Meaning?"

"That she won't be for long."

"Then Mrs. Bruce Mannering."

"Yes."

"Then you're not to be Mrs. Mannering junior? You're not Future Mrs. Mannering?"

"No."

"Interesting." He made tea.

"What brought it all about?" he asked quite conversationally as he poured and milked and sugared. It could, Gemma thought, have been a discussion on the weather. "Did Miss Stockley spill the beans on what happened that night?"

"Nothing happened."

"But did she?"

"No."

"Then—?"

"We just—well— Bruce and I simply—"

He nodded calmly. "You shouldn't have started it in the first place." He produced a packet of biscuits. "So it's all over," he said.

"It's all over," Gemma agreed.

"What next, then?"

"Back to Sydney."

"Via the Mitchells?" His brows had risen disbelievingly on her.

"I just wanted to see Harriet once again."

That seemed to silence him a moment, almost as though he had expected a different answer, and evidently he had, for he said: "I thought you might have learned I was here." When she didn't change her reply, he laughed drily, and asked:

"Will you get your old job back?"

"I don't think so. It was a highly competitive post, and there were plenty ready to step into my shoes."

"So it's the Positions Vacant column?"

"You could say that."

"Only I'm not saying it." He had taken out his makings and was rolling a cigarette. "But I am saying this: Instead of returning to Sydney, instead of looking up a room, then a job, how about considering me?"

"You?" she gasped.

"Yes."

"In what category? You must already have a book-keeper, a secretary."

"I have a whole staff of them," he agreed.

"Then?"

"Matrimony," he said.

Again Gemma cried: "You!"

"Am I that impossible?"

"No ... I mean, certainly not ... I mean, many women ..."

"But not you?"

She did not answer that. Instead she said: "Why this stampede all of a sudden?"

"Well, it couldn't be before, could it, not when you were the Future Mrs. M."

"But a thing like this takes—well, takes pre-thought."

Tim Torrance exhaled. "I can assure you that I have pre-thought."

"Is it to spite the Mannerings?" she asked curiously.

"Who are they?"

"Oh, don't be ridiculous, you know what I mean."

"Yes, I know, but I find your question in bad taste. I don't hold spite, and anyway, the Mannerings wouldn't rate even that much thought."

"But there must be a reason."

"I love you passionately."

"Now you're in bad taste!" she snapped.

"Please yourself about that. I'm told passion does enter into it, but if you'd prefer high regard—"

"Oh, don't be silly!"

"I'm not being silly, Gemma, I'm meaning every word, every syllable of every word. I want to marry you."

From somewhere inside her, for Gemma was not conscious of speaking the words herself, a voice, *her* voice, asked: "And for how long?"

"What do you mean?" His eyes were narrowed on her now.

"For how long do you want to marry me? As long as you wanted to marry—Jenny Lawson?"

He had put the cigarette down, so there was no weave of smoke to narrow his eyes, yet the eyes still remained slitted, estimating.

"What do you know about Jenny Lawson?" he demanded.

"I know she broke up her marriage for you, but after it was done that you didn't want her any more."

"So you know that," he said. He spoke very quietly, but Gemma could see that he was deeply, coldly angry, angrier than she had ever seen him before, and he was, she had learned by now, an easily angered man.

"Forget what I just said, Miss Glasson." He had risen sharply from the table, so sharply that the chair he had been sitting on fell back to the barn floor. He made no attempt to pick it up.

"You're like the rest of them," he said witheringly. "Ears sticking out to hear the worst of a man, tongue on the ready to flay him to pieces, claws sharpened.

But what am I complaining about? I should be thankful to you for letting me see your true colours before it was too late, the colours of all the female sex."

"Including Jenny?"

"No, as a matter of fact, *ex*cluding Jenny."

"Then why didn't you marry her?"

"Why didn't you find out the story first before you came to your own conclusion? And I thought—" He walked to the door of the barn, then walked back.

"Yes?"

He laughed sourly. "I thought you were different. I said to myself: 'Here's one who's different.' You're no different. You're run-of-the-mill. You may be ex-Mannering Park, but you're still imbued with their poison. Where's your ring?"

"Here." She was pulling it off, putting it on the table. "What are you going to do with it?" she asked. "You did say you would tell one of the men—"

"I'm going to return it personally. After all, it's a little too valuable to send over in a cowboy's pocket. No, I'll find Bruce and give it to him myself, I'll hand it over and say: 'Miss Glasson regrets, but by heaven, man, *you* shouldn't regret. You should kneel down and thank your lucky stars!" He had not got the last word out before Gemma, too, had risen. The blow she caught him across the cheek surprised herself as well as Tim Torrance. She had never done anything like this in all her life, and she was deeply ashamed.

He had taken a step forward, and she braced herself. She had asked for this. She had acted like a fishwife.

Then he was taking her in his arms instead, taking her as Gemma had never been taken in anyone's arms, and certainly not in Bruce's, in all her life.

"I think," he said, and his voice was thick, "that this will hurt you much more than what you were expecting."

His lips came down on Gemma's.

Of course she had been kissed before. What woman of twenty-six hasn't? But this time it was entirely different. There was a fierce gathering to him. There were hard urgent arms. There was a curious sense of time racing up to her, covering all the usual preliminaries in the duration of one close fierce second. There was a wonder, even a marvel.

Then he released her, released her so abruptly that she stepped quickly back.

But Tim Torrance was not there to see her fall. He had left the barn, climbed into his truck and driven away from Boothagullagulla. Though Gemma did not hear him. When she had stepped back, she had caught her head on a protruding ledge, and after that she heard nothing more.

It was dark when Gemma opened her eyes, only to shut them quickly with pain. Her head ached abominably, and she felt weak and giddy and sick.

She lay there till morning. Somewhere outside the barn, she heard Ludy calling the chickens, and she tried feebly to shout out. But nothing passed her lips. She heard Harriet being talked to later in the day, but Harriet's barn was too far away for any call to penetrate. Gemma relapsed into semi-consciousness again.

It was not until the next morning that she was found. A stockman, needing something in that particular barn, came in, stared incredulously, then raised the alarm.

Afterwards Gemma was told how the flying doctor had been brought in, how he had examined her but found nothing broken. How she had been transferred to the homestead but not taken to the base hospital, since in the F.D.'s opinion moving her right away might entail a risk.

All this went over Gemma's head, her confused, only semi-aware head. She was conscious of a nurse the doctor had brought in, of Ludy coming anxiously to the bedside every few minutes. Once . . . or so she believed . . . she saw Janet.

Then at last clarity came back, and on the same morning came the Mitchells. Isabel Mitchell, whom Gemma had never seen before, yet could have, Gemma thought, having seen Chris, came running forward and at once claimed Gemma as her responsibility.

From then on the pain for Gemma eased. The confusion stopped.

She was with friends.

The Mitchells were wonderful people. Never once was Gemma asked why she had been found on the floor of the barn, what had happened to make her fall as she had. If anyone else had been there with her.

When Gemma offered a sketchy explanation, it was accepted readily. The Mitchells never mentioned Tim Torrance, so Gemma never mentioned him, either. She knew he would have to come to Boothagullagulla some time in the future, so decided she would wait until then. When the Territorian truck did arrive a week later, but with one of the Territorian drivers,

Gemma knew she could be spared the ordeal indefinitely, especially when Isabel said:

"We don't see Tim Torrance as much as we would like nowadays. He's a busy boss, and hasn't any time for social calls."

"He works quite often himself on the trains," Gemma heard herself saying. She added quickly: "Or so I've heard."

"Tim Torrance would never ask anyone to do what he couldn't do himself. He tries out every aspect, does it regularly. Ludy was telling me that Janet Willis visited you while you were ill."

"Yes. I can barely remember, though. Do you mind her having come, Isabel?"

"Mind? Of course not." Isabel smiled warmly. "Anyway, I've always liked Janet."

"How would she know about me?" But even as she said it Gemma remembered Tim Torrance's:

"Up here a wind will blow even a change of mind." He had added: "And yours is a change of heart."

"It's a very powerful wind," she said now.

"Are you all right, dear?" Isabel looked concerned.

"Wonderful." Gemma told herself she must watch her tongue. "Only I do worry about putting you out," she added.

"Putting us out? You were what I wanted but barely dared hope for." For some reason Isabel's voice shook, and Gemma wondered why.

"How do you mean, Isabel?" she probed gently when the woman did not explain.

Isabel moistened her lips, then looked at Gemma piteously.

"Chris," she blurted at last.

"Chris?"

"That month in Melbourne was not a holiday jaunt, it was not business. It was a—health check."

"Yes?"

Now there was a very long pause. In the silence, Gemma could hear all the things one does hear in silences. The tick of a clock. The drip of a tap. An idle breeze turning over a curtain.

"He hasn't long, Gemma." Isabel managed to say it quite calmly.

"Chris hasn't—"

"No. I won't give you details. They're involved medical terms, anyway, and I doubt if I could get my tongue around them. But it's final, Gemma. Three of the best doctors are agreed on that."

"Chris—" said Gemma again, and she bit her lip.

"He doesn't know," said Isabel presently. "It's not that he isn't brave. Chris is the bravest man I know. It's just that I wanted it that way. Besides—"

"Besides, Isabel?"

"Chris's memory is deteriorating, and will finally go. I was warned of that, and I can notice the signs already. He's still keen on things that are happening *now* ... the weather, for instance, he always took a deep interest in that, and he's now more alert there than ever."

"But the past is receding?"

A pause, then: "It's getting mixed up with the present, Gemma. You, for instance, sometimes become—" But Isabel did not go on with that.

"If the past had not forsaken him," she resumed presently, "if he could look forward to his Neroli soon, for, Gemma, I've never seen two people so made

157

for each other as were Chris and Neroli, it would be quite different. Chris could know. He could be told. But very soon he's not going to remember Neroli as she was, only" . . . a tentative look at Gemma . . . "as she is."

"As she is?"

"If we told him there wasn't long for him what would he have to hold on to, not remembering *that* Neroli, only knowing *this* Neroli?"

"This?" queried Gemma.

"He would be leaving someone," Isabel said unhappily, "not going to her. Do you follow me, Gemma?"

She left it at that. Then.

Janet visited the Mitchells again. She sat on the verandah and looked closely at Gemma.

"You really must have knocked yourself out, you still look pale. I expected you to be out of it by now. I expected the very relief of being rid of the Mannerings would put you on your feet again."

"I never wanted to be rid of you, Janet, and talking of how people look, *you* look wonderful."

"I'm having a baby." Janet gave a little secret smile. "And it's going to be a Willis. I don't know about that Deborah that Bruce has entangled himself with . . . oh, yes, it's signed, sealed and delivered now . . . but somehow I don't think babies will be high on Deborah's list. In fact I don't think they're going to appear at all. Which means that Mamma will be looking to me for future Mannerings. But *I* am having a *Willis*."

"Because you love Jim."

"Love that foreman!" But there was something in Janet's voice that there was no mistaking.

"Bruce is coming to see you," she said. "Will the Mitchells mind?"

"They never mind anything," Gemma assured her.

"Then he's coming."

Bruce did. He sat down and said awkwardly:

"I got your note, Gemma."

"And later the ring?" Gemma had been worried about that, the ring had gone, but in the mood the Territorian had been she hadn't known what to think. Had he returned it personally as he had said, said the things he had told her?

"One of the men brought it across," Bruce told Gemma.

After a while he said: "Deborah and I—well—"

"I know, Bruce, and I'm pleased for you. I think it's going to be very suitable."

"I hope so. She's a very remarkable young woman. In many ways very much like my mother." For an unguarded moment a look came into Bruce's handsome young face, a wondering kind of look.

The news of cyclone Clarissa approaching the northwest coast at Essway Harbour came as no surprise to the Mitchells. For weeks Chris had forecast it. He spent hours in his weather room, as Isabel called it, plotting sun rays, latitudes, longitudes, wind courses. He had expected Clarissa.

"After Clarissa the rivers will rise like they've never risen before," Chris told Gemma. "You think the Lucy is swollen now at forty miles, it will soon be a hundred miles across."

"And our great snake in the lagoon," asked Gemma, amused, remembering the legend, "will it also come out of its hiding to watch, bring up all its cooling water and spread as well?"

"And spread and spread," sighed Chris. "Come and I'll show you how, Neroli."

. . . Neroli. There was a sharp edge in the room after Chris said that, but Chris was unconscious of any tension. Only Gemma felt it.

She crossed to Chris and listened to him telling her wind velocity, expected tides, cloud formation, all the rest, and all the time not hearing a word.

. . . Neroli.

That evening she told Isabel. She said simply: "I'm Neroli, Isabel."

"Yes, dear, I expected that."

"Isabel, what do I do?"

"He's my twin, he's my half, how can you expect me to answer for you, Gemma?"

"I could tell him."

"Yes, you could."

"On the other hand . . ."

Isabel said eagerly: "I was hoping you would say that. Oh, Gemma!"

Clarissa reached Essway Harbour one early morning. It came with a force and a venom never before experienced. The radio remained intact, and it reported havoc and catastrophe. The entire town had been flattened, and evacuees were pouring south.

While Isabel fussed around and saw what she could donate in beds and blankets, how many evacuees, if asked, she could accommodate, Chris showed "Neroli" in his weather room how every inland river now would rise, how every lower spot between here and Essway must feel the impact of swollen waters.

"Also our snake," Gemma said.

"That's aboriginal lore," nodded Chris, "but I believe there's something behind it, and that the underground waters will rise. I don't pretend to know the scientific cause, but I do know that our lagoon is fed subterraneously from somewhere."

"How long will it be a lagoon, Chris?"

"I don't know, Neroli."

... Neroli.

"I only know," went on Chris, turning to Gemma and taking her hand, "that we must face it together. You, Neroli. You and I."

"Yes, Chris," Gemma said gently.

Gemma let him keep her hand in his. When Isabel came in soon after, Chris said:

"Neroli has just indicated something very wonderful to me, Isabel. She feels the same for me as I feel for her."

"Then that's wonderful, Chris," Isabel said, but her eyes went to Gemma, and they were blurred with grateful tears.

"Thank you," she whispered when she could.

Though the cyclone was miles away on the coast, Boothagullagulla still received a share of the impact, and it was severe enough to make Gemma shudder when she thought of how frightening it must have been up there in the "eye".

The first warning was rain, loud, deafening, bursting rain that fell without any preliminary showers on the iron roof. It could have been a million demons, Gemma thought, every demon bearing wet violence in the form of vicious drops as sharp as javelins. It came down in sheets. You could hear the roof shudder at the heavy impact. Even the lesser drops that managed to push beneath the shuttered windows were still like stilettos.

Then the wind began. Even though everything was shut and barred, it still got in. It sent papers flying, curtains billowing, scattered flowers from vases, then, growing more savage still, even crashed the vases.

It thrashed the rain under every door, under every window, no matter how strongly secured. Once, when Gemma caught up enough courage to look out, she saw that the rains that had covered the lawns with mirror-like sheets were now wind-shattered into a million glassy pieces.

But she only saw it for a moment. The next moment it, and everything else, was darkly obscure.

Three of the windows smashed in and the noise was deafening. They could hear roofs being grabbed away, buildings dismantling.

"The men will be all right, though," Isabel assured her, "they would all make for the old stone barn, nothing will dislodge it."

"How about Harriet?" asked Gemma.

"They'll take Harriet as well."

Chris was their tower of strength. Weather had always been his passion, and now he anticipated every change of wind before it came, moved his women from room to room.

The deluge went on all night, but Chris said that in the morning it would have blown itself out.

"Mannering Park?" Gemma asked once.

"They would be getting it, too, of course, but not like this. We're in the direct line."

They bedded down that night in the room that Chris advised. Gemma thought she would never sleep, that the noise would prevent any sleep, but she must have. Probably through exhaustion they all must have.

They awakened almost at the same time, and it was dawn . . . and calm. No rain. No wind.

"It's over!" Gemma called.

"No, Neroli, it's only beginning." Chris was at the window, and Gemma joined him there.

At first she could not orientate herself. Everything looked different. Not different because it was smashed down, swallowed up, but *different*. She did not know where she was.

Then she saw that it was because of the water. There was water everywhere. They could have been on a ship . . . for a few minutes Gemma felt certain she was on a ship. Why, there were even islands . . . islands with cabbages growing on them. But they were not islands, and they were not cabbages, and she realized that. They were higher level paddocks, and the "cabbages" were tree tops.

All kinds of things were floating in the water. Uprooted shrubs, a garden seat, a small shed that had dismantled. The current was so strong in places that Gemma saw it suck in a blown-off roof and bear it rapidly away.

"What about our lagoon?" she asked.

"All this is running into it," said Chris, "and then there'll be the subterranean flow rising up in it, too. It will soon be an inland sea."

"A little more," said Gemma a little unsteadily, "than the great snake anticipated."

"Or I anticipated." Chris's face was grave. He reached for Gemma's hand and held it.

"But we'll come through, Neroli," he promised.

"A little paler," said Gemma, a little uncertain
on the over-like seriousness.

CHAPTER ELEVEN

THE telephone had long since ceased to function, but
Chris had always been able to contact his men's quarters and outhouses by a private system of his own
making. He had been one for tinkering even as a
small boy, his twin recounted to Gemma as she fussed
around. There would be no evacuees now, more like
it *they* would be the evacuees, but Isabel still had to
think about other people, and to prepare.

Fortunately the home phone was still operable, so
Chris rang his men, since the line was from homestead
to quarters only and not reversible so they could not
ring him. The women stood by, eager to know the
position.

It was OK so far, Barney reported, but the water
was rising fast. What did the boss think?

The boss had an answer to that at once.

"Get going," he told Barney. "Don't waste any
time."

"But—"

"We can't leave. We're too far under. We're in a
slight saucer here, remember, but you should be safe
for the next hour. Take the biggest trucks, Barney,
they're higher from the ground, and if you begin at
once, the track out should still be passable. Tricky,
and you'll have to keep your eyes peeled for debris,
but passable."

"But—"

"Look, Barney, I'm not suggesting, I'm ordering. *Get going*. Our outward phone connection is dead. We're depending on you to raise the alarm for us, so for heaven's sake, man——"

"What about the stock?" Gemma heard Barney shouting through the home phone.

"You can't have much left in there. Drive what you do have outside right now. They're not fools, they'll climb to the highest spot they can find. But" ... smiling briefly at Gemma ... "find room in one of the trucks for Harriet. Yes, the calf. Now get going, man!"

Chris, Isabel and Gemma stood at the window and watched the evacuation. The water was almost up to the top of the wheels of the trucks, but it was still quite safe. That Barney was not happy over the arrangement, though, was evident by the way he kept on looking anxiously towards the homestead. At length, since his voice would not carry that far, Chris picked up the phone again, gave it some savage rings, then fairly bellowed into it when it was answered that if the contingent did not start at once he'd get out his shotgun and make them start.

Barney came back from receiving the message, and the first truck took off into brownish water broken by fallen twigs and small branches. By the time the final truck ventured out to join the contingent the water was swirling into small waves, and it was deep yellow. They watched it until it, too, like its predecessors, disappeared from sight.

The sky had grown bleak again. Lightning danced in the distance and there was a faint rumble of far-off thunder. Or was the thunder the engine of one of the trucks protesting at what was being asked of it, then finally coming to a grinding halt?

"Tea," Isabel said. They had let Ludy go. She had offered to stay, but her anxiety for her family had been very obvious. The last they had seen of her was on the third truck with her husband and her children. Isabel now put down the big pot.

How many times did they have tea that day? Every time a sense of failure encroached on them, a desperation, an urgency, Isabel called "Tea!" and produced the big pot.

The will-o'-the-wisp lightning continued, the distant thunder. And the hours dragged on.

But the water did not drag. It rose as steadily, thought Gemma, aghast, as though a giant tap had been turned on. She stopped making mental mark-ups, such as how far up a selected wall, how high up a certain tree, because it only frightened her. How fast, she wondered, can a flood rise? How high? Yet she knew part of that already. She had seen aerial photos of people sitting desolately on the roofs of houses ... some houses no longer showing at all. She glanced at Chris. Just now he was being swept along with the responsibility and the excitement of it all, but how long could it last? And even if his spirit kept up could his frailer body keep pace? She saw Isabel looking, too, and knew she was wondering the same.

The rain had paused, but it made no difference to the steady rise of the water. The will-o'-the-wisp lightning ceased, but the sky remained its dirty beige.

Gemma stood at a window disbelieving that the sheets of water that were steadily covering everything in sight actually entailed the terrain that had greeted her when she first had arrived here. Then it had been green-grey country, green from the last wet, grey from the bullock bush standing in twisted clumps in the paddocks. A green-grey world.

But now it was silver, the silver of the insidiously encroaching water. Even the dirty beige of the sky seemed to be altering to silver as well.

Feeling suddenly imprisoned, Gemma opened a door and went out to one of the verandahs. One of the bright chintz cushions must have been dislodged by last night's wind, and now it lay soaked and mud-encrusted on the bottom step. She went down to retrieve it, her feet wallowing in mud even at the top rise. When she reached the cushion it looked so soaked and dirty she decided to leave it there after all. She came carefully up again, noting, to her horror, that already one more rise was half covered. Why, at this rapid rate . . .

Now the air they breathed felt like a damp blanket, the windmill that had always fascinated Gemma was deeply implanted in water. It stood quite motionless in the wet blanket air.

Gemma looked next in the direction of what had been the lagoon, that shallow expanse of water fed subterraneously from some hidden source. The aboriginals said it was the great snake, she thought, and that whenever the waters soared or widened it was the great snake who did it. Well, the great snake was certainly performing now! The lagoon not only stretched as far as you could see, it was wave-capped, filled with discarded logs and newly dismantled green branches. Water, water, water. Water coming from nowhere, going nowhere.

A great splash took her by surprise. In her absorption she had not seen the huge truck arrive.

At first she thought she was looking at some prehistoric monster, and then she realized it was the contrived front end of an articulated road train. If there are thirty-six wheels to a train, her befuddled brain tried to work out how many are there to a front articulation?

Tim Torrance swung out of the high cabin.

Isabel and Chris must have seen Tim coming. They were on the verandah, too.

"Your trucks got through all right, Chris," Tim greeted. "But only just. It's no good out there any more." He nodded his head to what had once been a track.

Chris said: "Why in heaven have you come, Tim? You must have known you'd never get out again."

"I thought you could do with another man around the house. Well, aren't you going to invite me in? Put on the billy?"

"You were a fool," Chris said, but gratefully.

"A nice fool," said Isabel.

Gemma said nothing.

They all went inside again.

"My main purpose," said Tim Torrance over tea, "is to tell you, Christopher and Isabel, that you're not forgotten. A helicopter is on its way."

"A helicopter?"

"It's the only answer. There's no other way out. Also, there's a lot more water coming. This is only the start. Then you mustn't forget, either, that you have that freak lagoon to add its extra volume."

Chris nodded, but Isabel looked away. For the

first time Isabel looked slightly nervous. Before she had taken everything as it happened, but now she barely repressed a shiver. "I've never been in a helicopter."

"We simply winch you up, darling, it's nothing," Tim assured her. "It depends on how high the water is when we decide from where we winch you, and from the look of the rise it could be from the roof. But don't worry, don't get alarmed. It'll be a cinch."

With the arrival of Tim, something seemed to desert Chris. He lost his sense of responsibility, he lost the anxiety that previously had kept him going. He grew older, perceptibly older. He seemed only too eager to pass everything over to the younger man.

But with the shedding of the load he had been carrying, he also turned instinctively again to Gemma. He followed her wherever she went, sought her out, let his arm rest on her shoulder. At one time he even called: "Don't go without me, darling."

Across the room Tim Torrance stiffened, looked incredulously at Gemma, looked at Chris, looked back at Gemma, then wheeled and strode outside.

One hour later they heard the distant cut of the helicopter. By the increasing noise they knew it was coming their way. Tim was on the verandah already, waving a white cloth.

They saw the big bird hover. Several minutes afterwards a winch came down. As the water was still only top step high, there was no need to climb on to the roof, so Isabel at least was spared that.

Gemma was near Tim as the ladder descended. A man came down with the winch and Gemma heard him say in a quiet voice to Tim:

"Two only, mate, we've a load on already. Sorry, but that's how it is. Now which one first?"

Tim turned to Isabel. Isabel, pale and strained but trying to be brave, was helped in and borne up.

Now the ladder was descending again, and Gemma was saying in a low but distinct voice, distinct for the Territorian:

"It has to be Chris. You do know that?"

Torrance turned and gave her a cool look. "There is a traditional saying, women and children first."

"*It has to be Chris.* He's ill. Gravely so."

"Is that why you're being so sweet? Having lost yourself Mannering Park have you now set your sights on—"

"Be quiet! It has to be him. I'll explain later."

"Then explain later, too, to Isabel, Miss Glasson. She's in this as well, in this estate, I mean, and sister Isabel is charity-minded and may have other ideas. Though perhaps you've persuaded her to make *you* her charity." He paused. "Have you?"

"Put Chris on, please!" Gemma begged.

"I shall damn well do what I think is right."

The ladder was almost down now. Chris was being edged firmly towards it by Gemma. She was leaving no room for Tim Torrance to intervene. She was calling: "Next trip, Chris, and I'll be with you, dear. In just a few minutes. Not long."

She waited until the winch had left, then she quickly escaped to the other end of the verandah. She was shaking with anger. How dared he go on like this with Chris, with her? How dared he say the things he had?

She stood at the very edge of the verandah, so

furious she could see nothing at all. It was even a while before she *felt* anything . . . and by then it was too late. The weatherboards at the end of the verandah were giving way, slowly at first, and then the entire soaked, drenched top end of the balcony was collapsing drunkenly.

Gemma, alerted too late, tried to twist desperately backwards to safey, but everything seemed to be disappearing from under her feet.

Suddenly she was in water, her feet grabbed by some irresistible force. All at once everything went dark, but even in the darkness she was aware of motion, of everything sliding by at a furious pace, though it would only be her own body, she knew, sucked by the swirling waters. Again she tried to resist, to grab something, anything, to hold her back. Then she went dark as well.

Her next moment of lucidity was not long afterwards, but to Gemma it seemed like hours. Gemma opened her eyes and found she was tied with rope to the double chimney of the homestead, every cushion, every rug Tim had evidently been able to grab wrapped round her to make the harsh imprisonment less severe.

"The rope was to keep you there while I went up and down for provisions," Tim said, "in case we have a long wait. I didn't want to come back and find I'd grabbed you out of the water only to lose you again."

"I didn't jump in," Gemma told him dully. She felt she had to say that.

"In the drink?"

"Yes. I didn't do it to—to—"

"To escape me? No, I didn't think even you could

172

be as stupid as that. In your filthy temper you just went too far to the edge. I happened to see you as you fell and grabbed you in time. If I'd been looking the other way . . ." He made a final gesture with his big brown hands.

"Chris had to go first." Again Gemma said it. For some reason she knew she had to vindicate herself.

"Yes, I think you've established that. But perhaps you won't be so pleased when you know that the 'copter has signalled that the light now is too bad for any more rescues, meaning you'll have to spend the night up here with me."

"Still, better me than Chris," was all Gemma replied.

"That," Tim said without expression, "remains to be seen."

"What do you mean?" she asked.

"If you think," he shrugged, "I'm going to balance like I am balancing now on sloping iron, you are mistaken. When the time comes to sleep—"

"Sleep?"

"One of us will sleep at some time through the night, even both of us. At such time I wish to be secured as well. And" . . . a pause . . . "there's only one rope, so it will have to be a case of closer settlement. It seems, Miss Glasson, that this time you *will* find yourself hitched"

"Hitched?" she queried.

"Hitched. You've had rotten bad luck in the hitching game so far, haven't you?"

"I don't understand you," said Gemma.

"You do, though," he said. "First Mannering . . . or were there failures before him and he wasn't the first? ... and now Chris."

"You're mistaken there," she said. "In Chris."

"No, *you* are, if you think you're going to get away with it."

"Away with what?"

"With what usually comes with long looks and all the sickening what-have-yous you displayed down there in the house. My God, I've never been so nauseated in my life!"

"You're quite wrong in what you're thinking ... that is if you were thinking—"

"Oh, I was thinking it all right."

"You're wrong, then, though I still don't see why you are objecting. Chris is not old."

"Nor is he young. Also, he's only flattered by your attention, and don't try to tell yourself anything else, you mercenary piece. In his rosy daze, he can't see your wiles, he can only see—"

"See Neroli," finished Gemma quietly for him. She paused. "Chris thinks I am Neroli. It was Isabel who asked me to go along with that. You see, Chris has very little time left."

The man on the roof looked stupidly at Gemma for several moments as though he could not understand what she was saying. Then he ran his fingers through his hair, making it stand up quite ludicrously if Gemma had felt like laughing, which she had never felt less like doing in her life.

"Neroli ...." he echoed.

"Chris's dead young wife, yes."

"And Chris had been thinking—"

"Yes."

"So you—"

"Yes."

"And Chris—hasn't long?"

This time Gemma said No, then followed it all up with what Isabel had reported from the doctors.

"I've just made a fool of myself, haven't I?" Tim said in a low, shamed voice.

"You have."

"I made a rotten mistake."

"You did."

"Gemma—Gemma, move over. I'm coming up there, too. I want to explain—I have to explain. I have a hell of a lot to say to you—Gemma—"

But Gemma was not listening.

"It's coming back!" she called excitedly. "The helicopter is back. We're going off after all!"

Thirty minutes later they had been winched to safety, taken to some high and dry place and found billets.

Gemma's hostess was young and friendly. She could not do too much for Gemma.

She had her in bed in a very short time, then plied with hot milk to ensure rest.

"I don't even know your name," smiled Gemma gratefully, halfway already to sleep.

"Jenny," said the woman. "Now rest, dear." She went out of the room and shut the door quietly behind her.

"Jenny," thought Gemma exhaustedly . . . it had been a totally exhausting day . . . "Jenny. Where did I hear that before? Jenny . . . Jenny?"

Gemma slept.

CHAPTER TWELVE

MORNING came with an attractive breakfast tray
set with everything from fruit juice to coffee, toast
and marmalade. *And a small vase of Salvation Jane.*

"Tim told me you liked our Jane," Jenny said.

Jenny . . . Jenny?

"Is he here, too?" Gemma asked her pretty
hostess.

"Oh, no, he went somewhere else, and no doubt
by now is somewhere else again. That's Tim." A smile
at Gemma. "You know, I've got to know you quite
a lot through Tim."

"He comes here often?"

"Never fails to call in whenever he passes north.
Now have your breakfast, dear, while it's hot."

Gemma nodded, and found she was hungry. After
all, all they had had yesterday had been tea. No one
had wanted to eat. She asked Jenny, who had remained in the room, had she heard about the
Mitchells.

"Afterwards, dear, I want you to eat while my
offering is still edible."

Gemma smiled at her, and complied.

"You didn't bring any clothes with you," said
Jenny, moving around and taking up and putting
down Gemma's few things, "and I'm plumper than
you. But better too big than too small. We can always
take things in. That will be your job this morning,

Gemma, putting tucks here and there."

"But my own things should be available as soon as a truck can get through to the homestead again."

Jenny kept on picking up, putting down.

"Also," said Gemma, "I won't be here long."

This time Jenny did speak. "The Bitumen is cut," she said. "You'll have to wait until the overflow drains off. Why the sad look? Am I that bad?"

"You're wonderful, and that's the reason for the look. You simply can't want me around. Your husband—"

"Larry is cut off on the other side of the Bitumen. He would be relieved to know I have company."

"Is this a station, Jenny?" Gemma did not know where she was.

"Yes, but not the sort of station you're thinking about, it's a filling station, a very important thing up here where the gas stops can be hundreds of miles apart."

"We're on the highway?"

"Just now" . . . ruefully . . . "we're on an island, and the highway is somewhere out there." Jenny pointed and laughed. "But don't worry, it runs off quickly, not like—" But she did not finish that.

"How would Tim get through? You said you thought he had."

"He would fly."

"That's what I'll do, then," decided Gemma. "As soon as I find out about the Mitchells."

"It may take you longer than you think," Jenny warned.

"Finding out about the Mitchells?"

"No." Jenny was quiet a moment. "No, that won't

take long. But getting away will. Even after you emerge from being marooned, there'll be a queue-up of travellers wanting to fly south."

"But if Mr. Torrance—"

"He would see to it that he went first." Jenny's voice held pride.

Gemma was quiet a moment.

"Was I brought here to you," she asked Jenny presently, "because you do good things like this? Like taking in stranded people?"

"I would take them in, of course, everyone up here would, but Tim came to me at once with you."

"I don't remember."

"No, you were practically out to it, poor dear. Timothy could have put you in a rabbit warren and you wouldn't have noticed."

"But he didn't, he brought me to Jenny's."

Jenny . . . Jenny?

"What comes after Jenny?" Gemma asked at last.

"Jenny Webster."

No, it meant nothing. Gemma decided not to try any more.

"What is it like outside?" she asked.

"Clear." Jenny seemed to be hanging back for some reason, Gemma noticed. "There's quite a lot of blue in the sky, but the water is still coming, of course."

"How long will it come?"

"Until all the sources are exhausted. It's really a wonderful thing, it's just that in some places . . ." Jenny's voice trailed off. "But," she went on at once, "it's marvellous to see the shrunken dams swell out again, the dry waterholes fill up, the windmills have something to turn round for. Drought is a horrible thing."

"Worse than flood?"

"I believe so, Gemma, even though—" Again Jenny did not finish.

"It was a brooding sort of day yesterday," Gemma sighed. "Almost like a wet blanket. Is it again now?"

"No. All that's over."

"I'll get up, Jenny," she decided.

"Yes, I suppose you'd want to. But before you do—"

Gemma looked quickly up. She had heard a different note in the woman's voice. "What is it?" she asked. Then she asked instinctively and at once:

"Is it Tim?"

"Oh, no, he's all right. I don't know where he is, but he'll be all right. It's—the Mitchells."

"But they're all right, too. We saw them leave on the 'copter. Isabel was nervous but very pleased with herself and her daring. Chris was too tired to care. But they're—all right."

Jenny sat down on the bed beside Gemma. She found Gemma's hand and held it in hers.

"The helicopter crashed," she said quietly.

"Oh, no!"

"It happened quite soon after it left you. You would even hear the noise, but would put it down to one of a hundred things that were happening all at once out there."

"Did Tim know?" asked Gemma.

"Not till he came in with you."

"But he said that there'd been a signal that the light was too bad for another rescue."

"There was a signal, but it wasn't for that. It was for—" Jenny bit her lip. "Afterwards," she said, "another helicopter did get you off."

"In the first helicopter, were they—were Isabel and Chris—"

"The 'copter crashed," repeated Jenny. "It was everyone, Gemma. There were a married couple and their baby, too, they'd only come north a month ago. And the pilot. And his helping hand." She sighed.

There was a long silence in the room. Gemma looked without reality towards the window. She could not believe it. She felt she never would.

"Twins," inserted Jenny gently, "shouldn't be parted."

"Perhaps you're right." Isabel, Gemma was thinking, in pain because of what lay ahead for Chris, her twin. What had she said? Her half.

"What about Boothagullagulla?" she asked at last.

"It's completely inundated. Not even a sign of the homestead or of any of the barns. Nothing but water. It will be like that for a long time, the experts say. The subterranean source is still disgorging."

"The great snake," smiled Gemma sadly.

"Yes." Jenny smiled sadly back. "Chris Mitchell's great snake waking from his long rest at last."

She left Gemma after that, and Gemma lay back trying to realize things, trying to accept them, put them in perspective, but it was hard.

At last she got up, put on the likeliest dress that Jenny had left for her, then went outside.

They were, she saw, on a veritable island. Evidently the service station occupied the highest spot for miles, for everywhere else was water. Evidently, too, Tim had brought her to Jenny just in time, got out himself in time, though the Bitumen, which Gemma could faintly decipher to the left, was draining off quite quickly, as Jenny had said. Gemma could even see, if indistinctly, the ink blue surface of the road.

She sought out Jenny and found her in the kitchen.

"Tell me other things," she begged. "I have to know."

"Not much more to tell, but ask me, anyhow."

"What about Mannering Park?"

"It took a battering, but it came through with everyone safe. All the other places did as well, Bellbrae, Everham, Two Gums, Blue Bush."

"You seem to know them, Jenny," commented Gemma.

"I should do, my father had a holding here. I'm a Top End girl. Then when I married" . . . a pause . . . "it was to a local man, as most of the girls do marry."

Gemma nodded. Jenny, she was thinking again, Jenny?

"Jenny Lawson." She said it aloud, only half recognizing her own voice.

"Yes, I was Jenny Lawson once. It was before I remarried. I married Larry." Jenny was looking closely at Gemma. "But, of course, you know all that."

"I don't . . . I mean . . . yes, Jenny, I have heard."

"Certainly you've heard. Up here, Gemma, it's no different from anywhere else. We have our own little intrigues, our own little suspicions and gossips. I was the topic of one of those gossips."

"And—Tim?"

"And Tim," Jenny agreed. "I think," she said after a few moments, "you'd better tell me your version, Gemma."

"Not mine," explained Gemma, "but as told to me."

"By a Mannering, no doubt. But please go on. I can take it."

"There's nothing to take, Jenny. I mean, nothing against *you*." Gemma was remembering Janet's: "She eventually got rid of her husband. He was a pig, and I don't blame her."

But after that, when Gemma had asked: "Through evidence with Bruce?" Janet had laughed:

"Oh, heavens no, through the Territorian. After encouraging her to go ahead, he faded out. Poor little girl left high and dry. There was quite a scandal."

"No, nothing against you," Gemma repeated to Jenny.

"I know," nodded Jenny, "all the venom went on Tim, and he wouldn't do a thing about it. Gemma, my first husband was no good. I could give you a lot of instances, but it's all past history now."

"How did Tim come into it?" asked Gemma.

"Among many other victims of Rod's dishonesty ... yes, his name was Rod ... was Tim. Tim called at our place one day to see Rod, and Rod" ... she bit her lip ... "and Rod—"

Gemma said quickly: "It doesn't matter, Jenny."

"But it does, because I want you to understand. Rod was being cruel. He was often cruel."

"You mean—physically cruel?"

"Yes. Tim came in and—well, it was the beginning

of the end. No, it was the end, really. Tim threw Rod out—literally threw him. When Rod acted legally against me later, he cited Tim, and Tim just let him."

"Yet—"

"Yet there was nothing, nothing except a man who couldn't stand by and see a woman hurt. I told him I was making a public announcement, and do you know what he did? He laughed. He said it meant as much to him as water on a duck's back, and Gemma, I believed him. He wasn't affected at all. At least, not until—"

"Yes?"

"When he left you with me last night, he said: 'Mind her, Jenny, the Mannerings as well as the flood have been at her. You know what I mean.'"

"And you know?"

"Yes. I knew they'd been saying what was untrue. For it was untrue, Gemma. Tim Torrance never cared one iota about me. I don't think he would have even looked at me had he not walked in that day."

"But you, Jenny?" Gemma asked carefully.

"Oh, I loved him. I still love him, will always love him. He brought me back to life, and he brought me Larry. Larry was one of Tim's men. When Tim saw how it was with us, he set Larry up here. He said a thirty-six-wheeler was no place for a family man." Jenny laughed.

"And is there to be a family?"

"Of course. And the first son will be Timothy. And what will the Mannerings, and all their friends, have to say about that?" Jenny laughed . . . and suddenly Gemma was laughing, too.

"After a penguin at a white dove party," she pointed out, "there's little left to say."

It was a week before the water drained away sufficiently for the cars to come through again.

First of the long contingent from the south was Larry Webster, anxious to be back with his wife again.

He reported the Bitumen as perfectly safe once more, in perfect condition for wheels of all sorts, from four to thirty-six, a fact that left Gemma frankly wistful for her small car still under water at Boothagullagulla. She had rung for an air passage south, but had been told that there were still many applicants before her, and she felt she was intruding now on a tender reunion. Larry denied the intrusion part, but he did come up with the bright idea of providing Gemma with one of the garage models.

"I want it taken down to Sydney," he said, "and you'd be helping me no end."

"You would also be getting rid of me before another week," laughed Gemma. "No, I know you didn't mean it that way, Larry, but I just couldn't help saying it. Of course I'll take the car down. It's the least I can do."

There was nothing else to wait for. There was still no question of going out to Boothagullagulla . . . perhaps there never would be, the inland sea that had arisen might never recede again. Not in this century. So—

So Gemma left the Websters in Larry's car to be delivered to Sydney, left after many hugs, many kisses and a few tears.

She was still wiping the tears away miles down the

Bitumen when she heard that imperious, demanding horn. Only one person, she thought, would accost her like that. She put her foot down on the accelerator. Last time, Mr. Territorian, I had only a small car, she was thinking, this time it's a fast model, and the race is really on.

But she might as well have put her foot down on butter. The thing passed her, every wheel of the thirty-six wheels splashed mud at her. And then, two hundred yards ahead, it slewed round and cut her off. The fool, the utter fool, she thought, this is the highway, this is the Bitumen just opened up again, ready to be used again, cars will be coming at any moment.

But, and Gemma would never know why, they did not come. Not now.

Only the Territorian came, slowly, almost indolently, as once he had come carrying in his arms a small bewildered Harriet, and saying:

"I have a passenger for you."

He said it again now, but she could see no calf. She told him coldly:

"This is not my vehicle, I'm delivering it for Larry Webster. You can't put any calf in the back seat of this car as you did with mine."

"Little Harriet," he nodded. "She's all right, you know. I checked on her. She's grown, and I don't think you'd remember her, nor she you."

"I would remember," Gemma assured him.

"You think so? Then you might also remember me. Name of Torrance. You might remember that I bought you a ring at The Alice." He waited a long moment, then:

"Why in heaven aren't you wearing it, girl?"

The ring. It was round her throat on a slender chain. It touched her heart. She had threaded it on the chain and put it near her heart the night he had given it to her. She had never taken it off.

"I took you to Jenny's," he said. "I know Jenny. You couldn't have stayed with her and not learned the truth. Jenny's all right, a great girl, but she still talks."

"Other people talk," Gemma pointed out. "Also they think. They think things they should never think. Like—Chris and me."

"I know. I know. But I could have killed you that day. You were tender with him, but for me you had only snarls."

"You couldn't have believed—" Gemma began.

"I didn't. Not really. But I tried to make myself. This wretched girl, I told myself, what's she playing me for?"

"Does anyone ever play you for anything?" Gemma disbelieved.

"Yes. Society, so-called, does. The nice, the oh-so-nice society you were engaged into, they played me as ruthless, forthright, greedy, overbearing—"

"Presumptuous, spiteful," finished Gemma. Bruce, she remembered, had used exactly those words.

"Well?" he asked. "Is it true?"

"You are forthright," she pointed out.

"Standing back would never gain me twenty trains, more than that of trucks, plus a fleet of little beetles to run up and down the Bitumen as trouble-shooters."

"Do you have to tabulate everything?" she said crossly.

"I just want you to know what you're getting, or"

... at a frozen look in Gemma's face ... "what you're turning down."

"Presumptuous," she chose next.

"Why not? Why shouldn't I presume I'm going to win you where others failed."

"You're impossible! I think it's really only achievement for you. Something to cap the Mannerings. Something to notch on your belt."

"And," he said quietly, "to notch on my heart. I love you, Gemma. I loved you the moment I brought a helpless calf to you and saw, in spite of your dismay, all the love in you that was waiting there. I had love in me myself, waiting, longing for an outlet. But it had to be for the right one, for a gem in a box. I knew it right then."

"Knew what?"

"Us, of course."

"But you couldn't have known."

"I knew," he said obstinately. "Now stay there. Don't move. There'll be cars coming through." He ran back and righted the road train.

When he returned he was still empty-armed. She asked where was the passenger he had asked her to take.

"Not born yet," he grinned. "I checked."

"But you said—"

"Yes, I said, but I wanted to shock you. 'Not all this again!' I wanted to hear you say." He opened the door and got in.

"You can have your—our—home anywhere you like," he told her magnaminously. "It doesn't matter. You won't be in it much, anyway. You'll be out on the road with me, aloft in a safe eyrie, no one to break

187

the fortress, and outside there'll be star shadows on the good earth."

"Star shadows are at night," Gemma said softly.

"So will we be there at night." He waited, then added: "In each other's arms."

A few moments went by, Gemma still dumbfounded.

"Hannah," he went on, "will look after our town house for us while we're gone. I've promised her that already. She's very pleased."

"*You* promised her?" Gemma gasped.

"Yes."

"But how did you know . . . how could you . . . well, how could you be so certain?"

"If persuasion failed," he said frankly, "I intended blackmail. I meant to tell a little story of a night in The Alice."

"But nothing happened in Alice?"

He looked at her implacably, then he said:

"It did, you know, in my heart."

She was half laughing, half crying. What a man, what a mad, crazy man!

"Yet successful, too," he reminded her.

"How do you know what I'm thinking? How do you always know what I'm thinking?"

"I just know with you. I knew something, too, that day when I saw you ahead of me going up the Bitumen, and I decided if there wasn't a blessed event to put me in your picture, I'd get in that picture all the same."

"How?"

"By throwing myself in front of you. Or by pleading thirty-six flat tyres. Or by leaning over and kissing you."

Which Tim did now.

"I'm twenty-six," Gemma said disbelievingly. It couldn't be like this at twenty-six, she thought, not achingly sweet, not beautifully crazy, not unbelievable like this.

"I'm thirty-eight," he replied.

"But you don't understand. At twenty-six you don't have rainbows. You don't stand on tiptoe. There's no cloud nine. And you're not swept."

"Aren't you?" he said, and he swept her to him and kissed her again.

There was triumph in his eyes, but there was also tenderness. There was conquest ended, but there was also adventure beginning.

He was pulling up the slender chain, touching the warmth of it and smiling at her for where she had put it. He was slipping the ring on her finger. Then—

There was a movement in the train, in the second articulation of the train, a bellow, a disturbance. The Territorian was out of Gemma's car in a flash... coming back before Gemma could follow what he was doing.

He carried a calf with him. Two sticky calf ears, soft and peaked and covered with downy gold hair and with insides of pink plush. A bewildered expression. An india-rubber nose.

"A bull calf," he told Gemma, "and that, for the *un*-future Mrs. Mannering, means that our second born is a boy.

"Mind him now, sweetest"... sweetest!... "or else he'll be trampled on. I'll pick him up when I meet you at The Alice.

"And Gem-in-my-box, while you mind him, mind

189

my heart."

Gemma nodded, and found words at last. She corrected:

"*Our* heart."

romance is beautiful!

and Harlequin Reader Service
is your passport to the
Heart of Harlequin

Harlequin is the world's leading publisher of romantic
fiction novels. If you enjoy the mystery and adventure of
romance, then you will want to keep up to date on all of
our new monthly releases—eight brand new Romances
and four Harlequin Presents.

If you are interested in catching up on exciting and
valuable back issues, Harlequin Reader Service offers a
wide choice of best-selling novels reissued for your
reading enjoyment.

If you want a truly jumbo read and a money-saving value,
the Harlequin Omnibus offers three intriguing novels
under one cover by one of your favorite authors.

To find out more about Harlequin, the following
information will be your passport to the Heart of
Harlequin.

information please

All the Exciting News from Under the Harlequin Sun

It costs you nothing to receive our news bulletins and intriguing brochures. From our brand new releases to our money-saving 3-in-1 omnibus and valuable best-selling back titles, our information package is sure to be a hit. Don't miss out on any of the exciting details. Send for your Harlequin INFORMATION PLEASE package today.